THE MAN WHO TALKED TO THE WIND

THE MAN WHO TALKED TO THE WIND

AND OTHER RATHLIN FOLK TALES FROM THE TOMMY CECIL ARCHIVE

COLIN URWIN

The History Press

First published 2024

The History Press
97 St George's Place, Cheltenham,
Gloucestershire, GL50 3QB
www.thehistorypress.co.uk

British Library Cataloguing in Publication Data.
A catalogue record for this book is available from the British Library.

ISBN 978 1 80399 818 3

Typesetting and origination by The History Press.
Printed and bound in Great Britain by TJ Books Limited, Padstow, Cornwall.

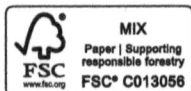

MIX
Paper | Supporting
responsible forestry
FSC® C013056
FSC
www.fsc.org

Trees for LYfe

Sea Call

The sea knows your name
Where you are
And how you came
To love the depths of it
The turning tides rise and fall
In all the dreams you dreamt
You heard its call
It flowed and roared
Across the axis of your heart
Into the dark blue lights of every wave
That captured your soul
The heaping waves upon the shore
You lingered by
Watching the mighty seabirds fly
Until you dived again to find
Your hidden world
The sea will not mourn for you
It knows your name
And where you are
Singing still
In deepest depths
And chanting waves
Its immortal song
For you

Mary Cecil

CONTENTS

FOREWORD

Almost half a century ago, a proposal I put forward to collect folk tales on Rathlin Island was accepted as part of my work programme. Equipped with my Ulster Folk and Transport Museum issue Uher tape recorder and a few essentials (which included a tent, as in those days there was no guest house or other tourist accommodation on the island), I drove to Ballycastle and caught the ferry, not entirely sure when I would be making my return trip. In those days, visits to Rathlin were even more heavily dependent on the weather than they are now. The trip took an hour. I watched spellbound as slowly we drew closer to the island and at last Church Bay was in sight.

My trusted, and usually infallible, method at that time for striking up acquaintanceships with potential storytellers was to go to the local shop, place my tape recorder prominently on the counter and buy myself a treat, usually a bar of chocolate. Inevitably, someone would ask me what the machine was for. I would explain my mission and was always directed to someone with a gift for narrative. So naturally, once my tent was pitched securely, I headed for the island's nearby shop.

My method failed me. No one paid the slightest attention to my recording equipment and eventually I had to explain to the young lady behind the counter my reason for being on the island. In a Scottish accent perhaps more marked then than it is now, she told me in no uncertain terms that there were books about the island I could consult. Swallowing hard, I responded that I had indeed read them, but I was hoping to learn about the island from the perspective of the islanders themselves, which didn't seem to me to be very well represented in existing publications. I was given directions to a nearby house and told to be there at nine o'clock where I could talk to her husband, who should be back from scuba diving by then.

By this time, my heart had sunk to my boots. I had been collecting folklore for about three years by this stage and unconsciously subscribed to the prevailing certainty that stories were the sole preserve of elderly gentlemen, which, unless this lady had married someone very considerably her senior, her husband could not possibly be. And what on earth would a scuba diver know about folklore? Furthermore, the lady's accent clearly revealed that she hailed from somewhere other than the island. I loaded a single tape into my machine, mainly out of politeness. At the appointed time, hoping at least that the person I was going to meet could send me on to a more suitably qualified individual, I presented myself at the house to which I had earlier been directed.

By the time I left it was the small hours of the morning and I was giddy with delight, I had been treated with much more hospitality than I could possibly have merited by the lady herself. I had learned how entirely misguided all my preconceptions were. I had met the totally astonishing, spellbinding Thomas Cecil and his equally remarkable wife, Mary. Best of all, perhaps, I had an invitation to return to the house a few evenings later. For that next visit, I brought an adequate supply of tapes and batteries.

That first trip was made in the summer months, but it quickly became apparent that, as Thomas had a vast repertoire, it would be necessary to return. The best time to do so would be in the winter when the weather would mean that Thomas would not be so busy with the demands of his diving work. That posed another challenge, for during winter it was very hard to predict when the ferry – which Thomas and his brother-in-law Neil also provided – would run. Mary kindly came to my aid. If I indicated when I might come out to the island, she would telephone and let me know when Thomas was going to operate the ferry. With this arrangement in place, I used to keep a bag packed and ready so I could jump into my car and drive to Ballycastle when Mary's calls came through.

I clearly remember one occasion when, in atrocious weather, Thomas needed to bring a bridegroom from the island to Ballycastle for his wedding. A call from Mary and I was on my way north to make the return voyage. It was the only time Thomas and Neil insisted I stay in the wheelhouse and that I saw charts unrolled and ready for consultation. In those days my husband, Ronnie, had working arrangements sufficiently flexible to permit him to be able to come to the island with me and we passed many, many memorable and magical winter evenings in the warmth of the home of Thomas and Mary: a warmth that was characterised as much by their personalities and kindness as it was by the glowing fire on the hearth.

Thomas had garnered his vast repertoire of narrative and other lore from his great uncle Robert and from other sources, including his father. As a young boy he had the presence of mind to record much of this in notebooks, but a great deal of it he had committed effortlessly to memory. It may seem strange that, for a storyteller, Thomas was not a man to waste words, and this was reflected in his spare, often laconic and always remarkably graceful narrative style. While his father never permitted me to record him directly, after I had visited the island a few times, he began to tell Thomas narratives that were to be passed on to me. I remember the first time I heard one of these, prefaced by Thomas with, 'My father said I could pass this one on to that girl from the museum.'

Academics have long debated the challenges of transcribing folk narrative so that it can be presented on the page in written form. Some have devised complex and ingenious methods for indicating cadence and other matters integral to oral form. In presenting Thomas' stories in written form, Colin has found a different solution and has given them a literary treatment. There are, of course, precedents, such as Hans Christian Andersen, for doing exactly this and Colin, who himself is well known as a storyteller, has done it with elegance and skill. As he explains, the cadences of his written words are his own: one storyteller embracing the repertoire of another in a seamless way as the tales are transmitted in written rather than oral form.

Colin has also applied his own extensive knowledge of the island's folklore so that he and Thomas can join in collaboration to prepare the stories for publication. How I would enjoy it if I might be permitted to join them in one of those evenings Colin imagines. Meanwhile, as Colin explains, Thomas' stories themselves can be accessed in the archives held by the Ulster Folk Museum.

Among his selection of stories from Thomas' repertoire, Colin includes one he has entitled 'The Third Wave', explaining in his introductory note about the tradition on Rathlin of the third wave being the largest. Thomas assured me many times that he always counted the waves himself. He also told me of how long ago smugglers, when chased by the excise men, used to take advantage of a narrow gap at a certain place near the West End between some rock stacks and the island itself. It was only at the last minute that the gap would appear as from almost any vantage point the stacks seemed to be a continuous line of cliff along the coastline. The smugglers would seem to have vanished but instead had used their navigational skills to pull clear and escape their pursuers.

Thomas often promised that he would take me round the island by sea, and one jewel bright summer day he invited me to accompany him in his motorised dory. Of itself, this was an unforgettable occasion in an extraordinarily beautiful place, and that alone would be enough to fix it forever in my memory. At one point on our journey, Thomas cut the boat's motor and I thought he was just taking a few minutes to enjoy the tranquillity of the extraordinary afternoon. Then I realised he was concentrating with great intensity, and counting, almost under his breath. Silently, I began counting too, 'one, two, three: one, two, three …' A huge wave swelled under the little craft, and suddenly Thomas started the motor once more. The wave carried us toward what appeared to be a solid face of high and unforgiving cliff, but at the last minute a gap opened between the stacks, and we were through. Folklore made vibrantly real by a most remarkable person, a man one implicitly trusted with one's life.

Linda-May Ballard
May 2024

INTRODUCTION

Tommy Cecil (1946–97) was born and bred on Rathlin Island, just off the north coast of Ireland. The man was many things to many people. First and foremost, he was a faithful husband to his wife Mary and a loving father to his three sons and four daughters. He was a loyal friend to a few and well known by his island neighbours. Among his many colleagues and acquaintances, he could call on fishermen, sailors, farmers, artists, journalists, politicians, celebrities, and countless other individuals from all walks of life. To them he was a larger-than-life character who, even in his tragically foreshortened lifetime, attained legendary status. To understand the man behind the legend we must first visit his native island.

Rathlin, or the Enchanted Island as it is sometimes known, sits like a giant well-placed stepping stone between Ireland and Scotland. It is approximately 3 miles from the Irish mainland and 15 from the Mull of Kintyre. The island is a reverse L shape turned 90 degrees anticlockwise. It measures 4 miles long from east to west and 2½ miles from north to south. Its highest point, Slieveard, often referred to as 'the mountain' by islanders, is 440ft above sea level. Due to many factors, the population has fluctuated greatly over the years. During the Irish Famine five hundred people left in one day. At time of writing there are about one hundred and twenty-five souls.

The island was home to Neolithic people, who made beautifully crafted axe heads from porcellanite – a highly valued hard black rock found in only in one other deposit on the mainland, at Tievebulliagh in the Glens of Antrim. In 2006 a Bronze Age cist grave was discovered during building work at the island's pub. The grave contained human remains that carbon dating showed to be from about 2000 BC – a thousand years before the arrival of the Celts, who were widely thought to be the ancestors of modern Irish people. DNA analysis, however, revealed a genetic continuum with the Rathlin remains and today's population, and this turned the previously held archaeological theory and timeline on its head.

More than two millennia later and Rathlin was at the centre of the ancient Gaelic kingdom of Dál Riada. This realm ran from the north-east of County Antrim up to the Isle of Skye, taking in the Inner Hebrides and a huge swathe of the Argyll coast. For hundreds of years Rathlin and her resources were fought over by Vikings, chieftains and Sassenachs. Its ownership was long disputed between Ireland and Scotland and, in local lore at least, settlement was only reached by dint of the fact that, like mainland Ireland, no snakes existed on Rathlin. It was purchased from the Earl of Antrim by the Reverend John Gage in 1746 and an old Rathlin story goes that Gage, having got wind that a party of islanders were en route to do a deal with Lord Antrim themselves, purchased the island from under their noses (Ultster Folk Museum archive reference *R80.30.19/4/80*). In any case, Gage and his descendants owned Rathlin and largely controlled the fortunes of the islanders up until relatively recent times.

Many species of animal make Rathlin their home. The famous golden hare – a rare and distinct light-coloured, blue-eyed variation of the Irish hare – is found on Rathlin. All kinds of wonderful marine life from whales and dolphins to basking sharks often appear around its coast. Spectacular blue fin tuna and thresher sharks have both been seen and captured on camera in recent years. For millennia, tens of thousands of guillemots and gulls have come to breed on the cliffs at Kebble near the West Lighthouse, now an RSPB reserve. Once, in the not-too-distant past, the great seabird colonies provided islanders with a ready supply of meat and eggs. Nowadays, local people and tourists alike eagerly await the seabird colonies coming to life each spring. Puffins are a favourite with the birdwatchers and nature enthusiasts, who come from far and wide to enjoy the spectacle. There are other bird rarities including the once common corncrakes that have made something of a comeback after a few years of absence.

Like so many lovers of wildlife and wild places, I too was drawn to Rathlin several times over the last thirty odd years. In this modern era there have been some stark transformations, not least the removal of dozens of scrap vehicles and the building and renovation of numerous dwellings. The inhabitants have watched as their island home has developed from a neglected backwater into a thriving tourist attraction. As would be the case with any group of people, some approve wholeheartedly while others might have preferred to take things a little slower. One islander who was always eager to bring about positive change for the benefit of the whole Rathlin community, however, was Tommy Cecil. Well known for his vision, passion and dynamism, he could come across as more than a little pushy and argumentative. But if he held strong opinions he was not opinionated, and he was nothing if not a deliberate man.

At a time when the Northern Ireland 'Troubles' were raging on the mainland and some people were tentatively arguing that Catholic and Protestant children should not be segregated in school, Tommy Cecil, along with his wife Mary, were fervent advocates for integrated education on the island and demanded that right for their own seven children.

Besides being a busy family man and vigorous community campaigner, seafaring and adventure were in Tommy Cecil's blood. He was an avid scuba diver and in his youth he had been a deep-sea merchant man for a couple of years. Among other places, he sailed to Australia but having seen a bit of the world and saved some money he came back home to set himself up with a fishing boat and go into business with his friend and soon to be brother-in-law, Neil McCurdy.

Like all islanders, he had to be very resourceful. As well as fishing for lobsters among the wrecks that litter the waters around Rathlin, he skippered the island's ferry boat for over twenty-five years. He carried the island children back and forth to school on the mainland. He fetched men to their work and brought back the mail. He took pregnant women and medical emergencies across the Sound in all kinds of weather, day and night. Over the years he briefly touched the lives of thousands of tourists. Many visitors to Rathlin fell under his spell and fondly remember his great store of home-grown knowledge and wit.

For years Tommy relentlessly canvassed for better and safer harbour facilities, only for his efforts to backfire. The government eventually heeded his calls but in the process robbed him of his livelihood and put the ferry service out to commercial tender, for which his vessel could not compete. Badly mauled but not beaten, in the early 1990s Tommy opened his own diving centre on Rathlin. Just as the fishermen do with the central character in the title story of this book, *The Man Who Talked to The Wind*, visiting scuba divers, both novice and experienced, always sought Tommy's advice. His expert knowledge of the treacherous tides, currents and the wrecks around Rathlin (on which he published a book in 1990, *The Harsh Winds of Rathlin*) was second to none.

Some of the stories relating to Tommy Cecil's many exploits have passed into island legend. Like the time he appeared as a witness for the prosecution in a case involving the shooting of a rare bird by a visiting sportsman. The fowl in question was a chough – a red-billed, red-legged member of the crow family – which afterwards became extinct on Rathlin. Tommy gave evidence to the effect that while out rowing in the bay he heard a shot. Seeing a bird falling into the sea, he rowed over. Realising it was a rare and protected species, he collected the specimen, which was now offered in evidence to the court. During cross-examination, council for the defence put it to Tommy that since he had only heard a shot, found a bird and subsequently saw the defendant with a shotgun, he could provide no evidence of causality. Tommy considered this proposition briefly before commenting, 'Well, the chough didn't commit suicide by shotgun.' The man was convicted.

Perhaps Tommy was made most famous to the wider community for his role in the rescue of the billionaire businessman Sir Richard Branson. After crossing the Atlantic by balloon in record time and touching down briefly on Irish soil near Limavady in County Derry/Londonderry, the capsule carrying the tycoon was still being dragged along, dangerously out of control, by its huge balloon. Swooping low over the sea near Rathlin, it was spotted by Tommy, who set off in pursuit. When the capsule eventually ditched into the ocean Tommy was in position and managed to get a line on to it.

Next thing Tommy found himself in a potentially intimidating stand-off with a Royal Navy warship intent on salvaging the stricken craft. 'Let go your line Paddy,' an English sailor ordered condescendingly and followed with menacing threats when Tommy refused. Tommy took his camera out to record what might happen next. Only after an officer apologised and flashed the utmost civility did the indomitable Rathlin man back down and agree to relinquish his claim, saying, 'If ye'd asked me nicely in the first place ...' Before he let go the rope though, Tommy cheekily asked, 'You wouldn't happen to have a wee drop of petrol to get me home would you?' His request was readily acceded to.

Shortly after, Sir Richard Branson visited the Cecil family home, where he dined on freshly caught lobster and was warmly regaled by Tommy and Mary. Later Sir Richard generously donated £25,000 towards the refurbishment of the Rathlin Manor House and funded a high-speed inshore rescue vessel for the island. During its maiden voyage from Ballycastle across the Sound, Sir Richard and accompanying journalists held on for grim death. Proudly at the helm was Tommy Cecil deftly steering the small craft over the waves at terrific speed, seemingly oblivious to the sheer terror being experienced by all those on board. One photographer was heard to sing 'Abide with Me'!

Much less well known off the island was Tommy Cecil's love and knowledge of Rathlin folklore. From an early age he had been exposed to the oral storytelling tradition that still survived into the 1950s and '60s. His parents and grandparents and his great uncle Robert McCormick used to gather with other islanders and lighthouse keepers to ceilidh – tell stories and gossip to pass an evening. Listening wide-eyed, sometimes when he should have been in bed sleeping, Tommy gained a huge repertoire of island folk tales organically implanted in his boyhood. He did write some down, which was frowned upon, particularly by his great uncle, but by his own admission he had probably forgotten many more than he remembered.

Though clever and naturally questioning, Tommy was superstitious in ways some might now find absurd. For example, he would not allow playing cards in his house – a common enough taboo in Ireland even yet. He had been brought up with stories where the Devil or some other malignant spirit often appeared when cards were being played. But he had also once had a strange experience himself and did not shy away from talking candidly about it.

While at sea years before, he travelled to the Far East. During the voyage a crewmate had been involved in some sort of violent altercation ashore and been killed as a result. Later, as his ship was ploughing through the Indian Ocean, Tommy was playing cards, as the men often did to pass the time. In the middle of the game, he went back to his cabin and walking along the passageway encountered the apparition of his young dead crewmate coming towards him. Tommy rubbed shoulders with the ghost and distinctly recalled the sensation of the physical contact. Associating this strange happening with the card playing, and probably remembering the old stories from his youth, he never again touched the 'devil's cards', nor would he suffer them under his roof *(R80.30. 19/4/80)*.

Another unusual incident highlights Tommy's acceptance of what some might describe as superstition. One summer, his uncle was visiting the island from the mainland. They were out fishing in a boat enjoying the fine weather when Tommy heard seals calling. It was an unearthly wailing and moaning not normally heard during the day or at that time of the year.

'Damn, but isn't that funny, do you hear the seals?' he said.

'I can't hear them,' said the older man.

Tommy stopped the engine. The sound of the seals came clearly across the water to his ears, but his uncle heard nothing. That evening Tommy's uncle was walking down the road and had stopped to talk to some other relatives when he suddenly dropped dead. His heart had given out. Tommy firmly believed that the calling of the seals that went unheard by his uncle was a foretelling of his death.

It was in the summer of 1979, and periodically over the next two and a half years, that a folklore collector called Linda-May Ballard from the Ulster Folk and Transport Museum visited Rathlin several times to record Tommy and other islanders he introduced her to. But for Tommy's intervention in this respect the other older islanders may not have cooperated so freely with Ms Ballard for they were deeply distrustful of her likes. In the 1950s Mary Campbell had taken down stories and folklore and in her book, *Sea Wrack*, later represented the islanders in ways they did not approve. In the end, Ms Ballard won them over and gained their confidence and friendship to record a remarkable archive.

Listening to the tapes and reading the manuscripts made by Ballard forty-odd years ago, it is clear she was taken with Tommy Cecil (TC) and became very fond of him – how could she not be, for he was such a good host and a naturally enchanting storyteller. In turn she was welcomed into the Cecil household like an old friend and was trusted implicitly. Ancient stories dating as far back as the time of the Viking raids on Rathlin were recorded, as were countless anecdotes and little scraps of tradition, myth and legend. Ballard's legacy and that of Tommy Cecil is a wonderful record of material that might otherwise have been lost forever. Instead, it offers us a rare glimpse of a way of life long since faded and gone.

As a storyteller and lifelong lover of local folklore, I only became aware of this collection held in the Ulster Folk Museum a few years ago. Since then, I have gleaned one or two stories from it through other storytellers. In 2022 I was commissioned by the Causeway Coast Museum Service to research and write an anthology of folk tales originally collected by Coleraine man Sam Henry in the 1930s; mainly, it is believed, from another Rathlin storyteller called Katie Glass (referred to by TC).

The book came to be titled *The Iron Hag and Other Stories from the Sam Henry Collection*. It was my great pleasure and privilege to breathe life back into these old stories. To promote and freely distribute the book I returned to Rathlin in the summer of 2023 and shared a few of the stories from it to a small but enthusiastic gathering in the Manor House. Afterwards I was approached by audience members with interesting questions and anecdotes of their own. A few requested to have the book signed. At the very end a woman came up to me. She was clutching a copy of the book and when she spoke I detected the twang of a Scottish accent.

'You won't know me,' she said quietly. 'My name is Mary Cecil.'

'I know we have never met,' I said, 'but I know exactly who you are.'

We exchanged a few more pleasant introductions and then Mary took the bull by the horns and asked the question that had formed in her mind.

'Could you do the same with Tommy's stories – that you did with Sam Henry's?'

I needed no time to consider the request and answered without the slightest hesitation.

'I would be absolutely honoured to do so,' I said.

There and then I pledged to bring together, rewrite and reimagine Tommy's stories and publish them in a book to his memory. How many there were and exactly how this might be done I gave not a moment's thought. I corresponded with Mary a few more times and visited the island again in late 2023. She gave me the transcripts of the recordings made by Linda-May Ballard, and I spent some time with her gaining a much better sense of the man whose life and stories I would soon immerse myself in.

She told me about the recording sessions that had taken place in her home. They were recalled as evenings of mirth and magic that had not been experienced for many years on the island. She recounted humorous anecdotes of Tommy's antics and adventures. Her tongue-in-cheek exasperation often appeared but it was her immense pride for all her husband had achieved and stood for that was most plain to see.

Inevitably our conversation drifted towards more tragic events. Mary told me about the day Tommy's older brother was lost at sea. It was in January 1983. Vincent Cecil was ferrying a government inspector across the Sound. Halfway over, his boat developed some kind of catastrophic failure and lost power. Moments later, Vincent, who could not swim himself, thrust the only lifejacket on board into the hands of his passenger. 'Put that on,' he ordered. Shortly after, the small vessel was inundated and the two men went into the freezing winter sea. The passenger was rescued and survived. Vincent's body was recovered a short time later. His selfless conduct was the mark of the man and for it he was bestowed a Carnegie Hero Award. Grief-stricken as he was, Tommy expected no less from his brother for they were both cut from the same stout-hearted cloth. It was a terrible blow for the entire family and most painfully felt by Vincent's wife and two children.

Fourteen years later, the Cecil family was struck by tragedy once again. It was 21 September 1997. Tommy was guiding a deep-sea dive on a wreck near the Scottish island of Islay, just a few miles north of Rathlin. Mary had not wanted him to go. He and one of the party were forced to make an emergency ascent from depth, resulting in Tommy suffering an attack of the 'bends' – decompression sickness.

He was flown by a military helicopter to a special decompression facility at Oban in Scotland but on arrival was pronounced dead. Tommy Cecil, the flamboyant man of action everyone thought indestructible, was gone. A light went out on Rathlin that day for the island lost its greatest and most outspoken champion.

Less than a decade earlier, on the eighth day of the eighth month in 1988, on the day Mary gave birth to the couple's youngest son, Tommy Cecil converted from the Roman Catholicism that he had been born into to become a follower of the Bahá'í Faith. He was attracted by the Bahá'í concepts of the oneness of God, the unity of humanity and freedom from prejudice. It might seem odd that a man who was so deeply connected to the ancient lore and traditions of his native island could make such a momentous sea change. At a time when Northern Ireland was starkly divided, and one was either a Catholic or a Protestant, Tommy's decision marked him out as the radical and deep thinker he was.

On the day of Tommy Cecil's funeral hundreds of people of all faiths turned out. There were fishermen and coast guards, divers and deckhands. Politicians of every hue attended. The Reverend Ian Paisley, the staunch Unionist leader and Member of Parliament for North Antrim, stood side by side with Baron Gerry Fitt, an equally staunch Nationalist, whose stricken yacht Tommy had salvaged many years earlier and for which he would accept no payment. Those who upheld him and those who opposed him were united in grief and respect. As the obituaries came rushing in, Sir Richard Branson described Tommy most succinctly as 'a man of courage and one of life's great characters'.

All this Mary told me without allowing herself a single tear or even so much as a trembling lip. I got the impression she had told the same story many times and had learned to control her emotions. It was abundantly clear to me that even after all these years she still mourned her husband deeply. It was a heart-rending and inspiring family history and, with everything I heard that day I, left Rathlin Island with my head swirling with a mixture of sadness, awe and admiration – both for Tommy Cecil and his widow of so many years.

Just before I took my leave of Mary Cecil, I told her I would be unable to open the huge envelope of material she had given me until the following spring. I had other performance and writing commitments to honour. I confess it took all my willpower to resist the temptation to steal a peek. Not until the beginning of March 2024 did I delve into the transcripts, and what I found both astonished and delighted me. The Tommy Cecil archive is quite simply a treasure trove of folklore the like of which I may never encounter again. I felt incredibly fortunate and slightly undeserving of such a privilege. Yet here I was poring over this wonderful and, in my view at least, highly significant collection of stories. It struck me that very few had been read or, more importantly, heard since Tommy Cecil last told them.

As I started work on the book in earnest I received a message from Mary Cecil, 'I hardly know how to start this …' she wrote. Mary went on to tell me she had been diagnosed with cancer and was soon to commence various treatments before undergoing surgery. We talked and during the conversation I found myself making more wild promises. 'You will be at the launch of this book Mary,' I said, with more conviction than perhaps I had any right to.

Having piqued the interest of a publisher, I now began to think we could not wait for the long-drawn-out process to complete. I began to write obsessively and, for a while, seriously considered having the book printed privately, thereby bringing forward its publication by a year. At the same time, I hoped that all this would prove to be unnecessary, and that Mary Cecil would not only be at the book launch but would live for many more years to come. In the end, the publishers were very accommodating and, under the circumstances, agreed to pull out all stops and speed up the process considerably.

I am very grateful to Mary Cecil for offering me the unique opportunity to write this book. It has been a great privilege. My sincere hope is that it will add another interesting layer to the memory of the man who inspired it. The whole community of Rathlin, not to mention the wider storytelling world and anyone with an interest in Irish folklore, owe a great debt of gratitude to the backroom and front-line academics and fieldworkers at the Ulster Folk Museum, and especially Linda-May Ballard, who possessed the foresight and skill to collect these last remaining stories before they were lost. Their true value may not yet be realised.

Special thanks go to Dónal McAnallen, Library and Archives Manager at the Ulster Folk Museum, Cultra, and his colleague Jonathon McBride. Their assistance has been unstinting and invaluable to me. I am indebted to the Arts Council of Northern Ireland for awarding the project a grant through the Support for Individual Artists Programme (SIAP). This has allowed me the time and resources to research and write the book.

To Nicola Guy, at The History Press, with whom I have worked before and hope to again, I offer my sincere thanks. Without her understanding this book would not have been published in such a timely manner. I would also like to express my admiration for the very talented Eileen Marie Emerson. Her illustrations are, as always, a delight and add so much to the atmosphere of the book. I thank her for her willingness to work on them under such pressure of time.

I cannot praise Linda-May Ballard enough for her dedication and professionalism in the creation of the Tommy Cecil archive. I thank her for her insights and knowledge so freely shared. Her suggestions have been very helpful. Most of all, I thank her for agreeing to write such a heartfelt and beautiful foreword.

I feel very fortunate indeed that so many people have been willing to put their faith in this enterprise and offer support and encouragement. I think perhaps the esteem with which Tommy Cecil was and still is held may have much to do with this. The last word on the subject goes to the team at Virgin Unite, the entrepreneurial foundation of the Virgin Group and the Branson family, who kindly reached out with the following message: 'We wanted to get in touch to send our regards to the Cecil family and wish you all the best for the project.'

In Ireland it is said that a person dies twice: once at the end of their mortal existence and again when their deeds fade from memory and their name is forgotten, never to fall from the lips of anyone again. That being the case, Tommy Cecil is destined to live on for some time yet. It is difficult to imagine a day when the island on which he was born, on which his children and grandchildren live, and for which he did so much will forget him.

I like to imagine Tommy Cecil would approve of my handling of these stories. In my dreams he and I would sit down over a pint of porter and discuss the whys and wherefores. Doubtless there would be robust debate, but Tommy was always a pragmatist and would understand, I think, that you cannot make an omelette without breaking some eggs! By all accounts he was not a self-satisfied man, but I imagine he would be quite pleased with what has been accomplished. I trust Mary and his family are.

I sincerely hope that people will enjoy reading and, moreover, telling at least some of the remarkable stories in this collection. If I have not done them and Tommy Cecil full justice it is not for the want of passion and endeavour.

Colin Urwin
April 2024

NOTES ON THE STORIES

There are over forty individual folk tales and anecdotes in this collection, though in some cases two or more have been combined under a single title, of which there are thirty-eight. There are a mixture of traditional folk tales, legends and myths, and one or two anecdotes Tommy Cecil remembered as actual events. I have made no attempt to categorise the stories but have simply set them down loosely arranged in what I hope feels like a natural flow.

In the process of reimagining and writing the stories for this book I have made many artistic and linguistic decisions, and in so doing have taken more than a few liberties. In the first instance, I had to invent a title for each story – folk tales don't necessarily have or need titles in the mind of the oral storyteller and TC did not seem to concern himself about such things. 'The Man who Talked to the Wind', as it was named, became the tale which I felt best encapsulated the character that was Tommy Cecil and so was chosen as the title story.

At the end of each story in the archive TC frequently finishes off by saying, 'So there you are', or something very similar. Every storyteller has their own style and winds up a narrative in a variety of ways. I have concluded most of the stories with something seemly, poignant or, for want of a better term, a punchline that in some cases sums up or crystallises the main message. In others I have just eased the reader or listener out of the story.

TC's style of delivery was that of the traditional oral storyteller. In this regard, he was the last of his kind. As opposed to the polished stage performance style widespread among modern professional tellers, his telling was conversational and direct. As such, it did not always translate easily to the page and much rewriting and editing had to be done.

Some of the stories required less 'fleshing out' than others but all were reframed to some degree to make them more accessible to the modern reader and appealing to the modern storyteller. In the case of 'The Headland of the Fair Colleen', for example, I took what was quite a spare rendering by TC (very similar to the one found in Mary Campbell's book *Sea Wrack*) and overlaid a more colourful version already well known and researched by me. Throughout this process I have drawn on my own general knowledge of local folklore and story and any misinterpretations are therefore mine.

Quite a few of the stories relate to Norsemen. TC refers to them as Danes and I recall this nomenclature was common when I was at school. Historically, however, the Vikings who frequently came to Rathlin were much more likely to be from Norway as opposed to Denmark. To avoid confusion, I refer to them as Vikings or Norsemen throughout. I use the term Lochlainn to refer to land occupied by the Norse – i.e. Shetland, Orkney and other lands to the north.

In 1746 the Reverend John Gage bought Rathlin Island from the 5th Earl of Antrim. In so doing he became lord and master over its population. Many are the stories of his and his successors' deeds and doings on the island, but Tommy Cecil never differentiated between any of these individuals. Here Gage appears as an amorphous character representative of the friction that existed more widely between rich and powerful landlords and downtrodden peasant tenant farmers. Similarly, there are a number of stories spanning many generations where unnamed priests appear, sometimes as a champion of the poor folk and at others as a more unsupportive or tyrannical figure. Doubtless there were frictions between islanders and their clergymen regardless of denomination.

Where no names exist in a written or collected version of a folk tale, I would tend to attribute suitable monikers to the characters I am reimagining – it makes the job of writer and oral teller easier, I think. Here, however, I have done exactly the opposite. In most of the stories TC did not use names. Sometimes, however, he quoted family surnames still common on the island, but he seemed anxious that such references should not be made public. Not being an islander, it is difficult for me to judge to what degree his sensitivity was genuine and necessary or tongue-in-cheek. Taking no chances, I omitted all first and family names, except Gage, which has been absent from the island for a number of years. Hopefully no one can or will take offence.

I chose not to use very much in the way of local dialect but did try to mimic TC's speech patterns as much as practicable. Only here and there have I included colloquialisms or sayings as I felt necessary and complementary. Always I endeavoured to keep the language as simple as possible.

In the 1950s when TC was hearing these stories from his parents, grandparents and grand uncle mainly, the native Irish had all but died out on the island. Even so, a fair amount of Irish words and phrases were freely scattered throughout the tellings. Not being fluent in Irish or taught the language in any meaningful way, TC seems to have occasionally misremembered names and inserted similar-sounding equivalents.

In the opening story, 'The First Monk', TC recalled the name of the monk as Banner – a name of English origin. This seemed rather implausible to me, and I took the liberty of replacing Banner with the Irish word *Deartháir*, which means 'Brother' and is pronounced *Jya-har*. This, I hope, makes more sense, and sounds a little more authentic. Likewise, I substituted and inserted other Irish names and words where they seemed most appropriate. I was ably assisted in this by my friend, native Irish speaker and storyteller from Galway, Mairin Mhic Lochlainn.

Towards the end of the recordings one or two stories were repeated by TC but with variations or corrections. In the case of 'The First Ravens', particularly, I thought the imagery and actions of the Viking characters in the first version more powerful and held closer to them.

I have included as much material from the archive as I could but there are many other little gems of local lore waiting to be discovered. I would encourage people to take advantage of the free and open access to this and the many other archives held at the Ulster Folk Museum. (At time of writing, the UFM collections cannot be accessed online via the British Library because of a cyber-attack, but this service will likely be resumed as soon as is practicable.) Each story here has a very brief introduction, at the end of which is included a tape reference number to aid readers who might like to access the actual recordings and hear the versions told by TC.

Colin Urwin

THE FIRST MONK

Fifteen centuries ago, the people of Hibernia – as the Romans called Ireland – kept faith with their old gods and religion. They told their own stories and clung to their old beliefs. But then came the new religion and Christianity inundated the land like a rising tide. Monks and priests took the place of the Druids. Christian teachings slowly subsumed the ancient ways and on Rathlin it was no different. This island version of events is, however, quite unique and interesting. (R81.57. 26/2/81)

Exactly how long ago it was no one now recalls, but one fine day a young Christian monk drew up his currach on to the shore of Rathlin. He called himself Deartháir – Brother – and took up a dwelling at place called Tareney – long said to be the site of the first monastery on the island – and there he lived among the islanders in peace.

At first the people were wary of the stranger, but soon they became a little more trusting for he was gentle and kind, and always he helped his neighbours with a heart and a half. The monk quickly learned all their strange island ways. He discovered they believed their dead went away to another enchanted isle far out across the western ocean to a place some called Tír na nÓg – a paradise where no one ever grew old, everything flourished in great abundance and happiness and joy knew no bounds. Only one or two favoured people had ever visited the much dreamed of isle and returned to tell the tale. But no one now remembered the last time anyone had dared to venture across the sea in search of the isle. It had become a mythical place but still it loomed in the minds of the people.

In time, the monk undertook to go and find this land for himself and vowed to return and tell the people all about it and bring news of their ancestors. This he did and the people were in awe when he came back with stories about the wondrous things he had seen and heard in Tír na nÓg. He went away again and again, but always returned and told the people how he had spoken with their long-dead forebears. He passed on dire warnings against this or good advice about that. The people listened, for just as they had always held their elders in the highest regard in life, now they hung on every word carried to them by the monk from beyond the grave. They trusted the holy man. He offered them something so rare and precious – the chance to commune with all those who had gone before. The monk was their window into the otherworld of which they had long dreamed.

The people began to beg for the monk's going away and eagerly awaited his returning. They craved his wise council. Through him, the people's ancestors sent word that they should turn away from their old gods and goddesses. 'Do not trust the Druids,' they said. The people did as they were told and slowly they began to accept the new religion and all its teachings. A few of the islanders resisted, but their voices went almost unheard in the clamour for the new ways. Once revered, the Druids came to be ridiculed and the old traditions soon forgotten.

In just a few short years the monk held sway over the people. He wrought change in every dark corner of their lives. He praised and chided them like children, and they meekly surrendered to his many strange rites and rituals. As the children cast their baby teeth they were paid to the monk like a tithe. He held them as a bond over each person and if, even as grown men or women, they sinned against his teachings or caused the monk any offence, which they always did, he would take their teeth and crush them into dust under a stone – a ritual that caused them great pain and mortification. As the monk's power grew so the people fell under his spell even more.

The monk, it was said, lived on Rathlin for a hundred years before he too died. The islanders buried him and said prayers as he had taught them. For a long time afterwards, no one ever ventured to the enchanted island again for the monk had never told anyone how to find it. In his time, the old wisdom and customs were all but banished. Like people all over Hibernia, the Rathlin Islanders became Christians. All their old high days and holy days were consumed by the new religion.

The monk was said to be a man of such virtue and holiness that he went, like Patrick and all the other saints and holy men, straight to Heaven – a place that was, by all accounts, not unlike Tír na nÓg, the Land of the Forever Young.

THE MAN IN THE MIST

The following narratives seem to be from more recent times but find their origins in the early Christian/Viking era. Rathlin folk tales that feature ghostly apparitions are, like everywhere else in the country, very common. Few ghosts are so helpful as the one featured here. (R80.14. 15/2/80 & R80.16. 17/2/80)

Years after that first monk came to Rathlin to convert the pagan islanders, a monastic settlement was established at a place called Killeany up on the north side of the island. Like most monasteries within reach of the Norsemen, it was raided. Year after year the Vikings came to Rathlin on their way to richer pickings on the mainland. They murdered any monks who resisted, stole anything of value and razed the simple monastery buildings to the ground.

When the Vikings left, the islanders often helped to bury the dead holy men in the monastery graveyard overlooking the sea. When the place was eventually abandoned and the monastery crumbled to a faint memory in the landscape, the graveyard became overgrown with nettles and briars.

More than a thousand years later, island farmers fenced off the rough ground, including the old burial place, near the clifftops. To keep their cattle from trying to break through the fences to get at the wild, salt-ladened growth, the farmers used to set light to the rank grass. No matter how fiercely the fire burned, the patch of nettles and briars that grew in the old graveyard was always untouched by the flames. Everywhere along the clifftops was burnt black but in the middle was a patch of greenery – the ground consecrated by the monks years before and where they lay in peace.

On some parts of the island the clifftops were yet unfenced, and it was not unknown for folk to get lost at night or in thick sea mist and fall to their deaths. People not from Rathlin wonder how an islander with his intimate knowledge of the place could ever get lost. But sometimes the sea mist comes in so thick that it can confuse even those who know the island like the back of their hand.

One night, just such a mist came in as a shore fisherman was returning home from a place called Dunagee on the north side of the island. The fog was so thick that the young man could barely see his hand in front of him. The fisherman was very loathe to tarry long for he knew his widowed mother was at home and would be fretting.

He feared she might venture out to look for him in the fog as she had done more than once before. Two or three times the fisherman found himself at the edge of crags. Another step or two and he would have fallen to his death. By now he was completely lost and had no notion of what direction he should go in to be safe.

Suddenly a shape appeared not far in front of him. In the mist he could just make out a figure dressed in what looked like a long overcoat.

'I'm lost. Do you know the way down?' he called, but no answer came, and the shadowy figure faded back into the mist. The fisherman called again, and the figure reappeared from the gloom. This time it was beckoning slowly. With faltering steps, the fisherman followed, and the same thing happened over again and again. The figure kept beckoning the fisherman on and he felt his way step by uneasy step.

Eventually he came upon a path that he knew well and would lead him to his own dwelling, and the figure disappeared for the last time. He talked with his mother and the neighbours, but no one had been out that night so bad was the fog.

In passing one day, the young fisherman told the priest about his experience and when he described the strange figure the priest thought for a while.

'Could it have been a monk's robe your guide was wearing?' he asked eventually.

There and then the fisherman realised that his guardian angel might have been the ghost of one of those long-dead monks from Killeany. Perhaps, thought the fisherman, one of his ancestors had helped to bury the dead monk all those years ago and the holy man was only returning the kindness. Whatever way it was, the fisherman was eternally grateful and every night he remembered the monk in his prayers.

THE OLD HAG OF RATHLIN

Even after Christianity came to Ireland the people remained deeply superstitious and, perhaps, even more prone to fear, intolerance and cruelty. Wise women or hen wives, who had always been so revered, and their ancient skills and knowledge relied upon by the people for everything from childbirth to preparing the dead for their journey into the otherworld, were oftentimes condemned. Prejudice swept Europe and tens of thousands of women were victims of the infamous witch trials of the sixteenth, seventeenth and eighteenth centuries. In Ireland women were not persecuted to anywhere near the levels seen even in Scotland and England. It is quite likely that the following story predates this era. (R81.57. 26/2/81)

It happened many, many years ago off the east coast of Rathlin that the people saw a wee currach struggling against the tides and the weather. Its bow was pointed towards Kintyre across the sea but for two days and nights it was caught in the stream, never able to make any headway. Whoever had their hand to the tiller did not know the tides. If the weather worsened, as was likely, they would be lost.

At last, a Rathlin fisherman could stand by and watch from the shore no longer. He ventured out to render what assistance he could to the little vessel. As he approached from astern he could see a small, lonely figure huddled in the boat. It was that of a woman with a ragged shawl draped over her head. She was moaning and weeping like a lost child. The fisherman hailed the stranger and when she turned he saw the tortured and lined face of an old woman. Her hair was grey and uncombed. She was staring back at him fiercely and there was hunger and fear in her wild eyes.

In an instant the fisherman realised the error he had made. He knew she must have been an old hag banished from the mainland for some evil doing, he knew not what. He wanted to turn his boat away there and then but feared she would lay a curse on him.

'Where are ye for in this weather?' he called through the wind.

'Cantyre,' she replied, never taking her eyes off the fisherman.

'You can't make it there. You'll be lost,' cried he.

'I'll be no loss to anyone,' sighed the old woman with a world weariness that would have brought tears to a stone.

The fisherman's heart softened and the cold fear that had seeped into his veins thawed a little. He took the old woman's currach in tow and brought her back to Rathlin.

'I was condemned as a witch and set adrift with no food or water. On the peril of my life, I was forbidden ever to return to Erin again,' said the old woman.

'Then you cannot stay,' said he, 'for if they find out we have given you food and shelter here on the island it would not go well for us.'

The fisherman and his wife cared for the old woman. They cooked fish for her and baked bread and they let her sleep by their fire. When she had recovered her strength and the weather turned more favourable, the fisherman guided her across the Sea of Moyle to Kintyre and put her safely ashore. As he bid her farewell, she called to him solemnly.

'If ever you or the people of your island need anything come to me. I will help you.'

The fisherman sailed away back home, glad to have rid himself of his strange visitor but sorry that he had left such an old frail woman alone on a distant shore to fend for herself.

Time passed and the people of Rathlin were attacked again and again by raiders from the north. Their crops and livestock were stolen. The men were killed or captured and the women raped. At last, the people remembered the story of the old woman from all those years before. The fisherman was sent across to Kintyre and there he found her scraping a living from the shore. She was even more haggard and ancient than before. He told the old woman the plight of the poor Rathlin Islanders and asked for her help.

'I can ease whatever troubles ye have,' she said, 'but here on this foreign soil or on the waves of the sea I have no power. If ye take me back to Erin my strength will come back.'

The fisherman had not bargained for this, but back to Rathlin he came with the old woman as his passenger. Great consternation was caused by her arrival, but the people agreed to let her stay if she could help.

'Take me to the place the Vikings make their landings,' she said.

As she stared down into the waters she ordered a fire to be lit and amid the smoke she incanted some strange words no one could make sense of. Her eyes rolled back in her head, and she wailed like a banshee. As she twisted her arms in the air and spun around, the people began to see a great swirling current forming in the sea. The waters churned and foamed, and from that day on it was impossible for a ship or even a currach to land there so strong was the current. Any that tried were swept away or dashed on to the rocks further along the shore. But for driftwood and seaweed nothing ever came ashore there again. For many years, no Vikings landed on Rathlin and the people lived in peace.

Their peace would have been complete except that there was one small price to pay. The old woman decided that she would remain on Rathlin, which was still Erin after all – the only place her otherworldly powers could be summoned. The people would have liked it better if she had returned to Kintyre, but they could not find it in their hearts to banish her for a second time. And so, very slowly they welcomed her as one of their own and she became known ever after as the Old Hag of Rathlin.

THE FISHERMAN
AND THE MERMAID

This is just one version of a very common story told all along the western sea-board of Ireland and Scotland and north up into Scandinavia. Variations include the sea creature being a seal-woman – a seal that can transform itself into a beautiful young woman (rarely a man) and vice versa, and known in Scotland as a selkie. On the north-east coast of Antrim, mermaids appear more commonly but occupy a similar folkloric position. (Ref. C79.29. 16/7/79)

There was once a very poor fisherman who lived on Rathlin. I won't mention his name, for his descendants live there yet. He had no boat and could only fish from the shore. One summer evening he went to the rocks on the north side of the island, where he had often been lucky enough to catch what fish would keep body and soul together.

While he was fishing he heard beautiful singing, but he did not recognise the air and nor did he the words for they were of a strange language. He was drawn to the music like a moth to a flame and then he spied a maiden sitting on the black rocks by the edge of the sea in the late evening light, singing away to her heart's content. She was as naked as the day she was born, and never in his whole life had the fisherman seen the like.

As soon as he clapped eyes on her he wanted her more than he had ever craved anything in all his born days. Long did he listen to the sweet singing, and he watched the young woman combing her long hair until he was completely entranced. But then he saw something that made his heart almost leap to his throat with fear and wonder. It was a long fishy tail with great fins that she raised as she moved on the rock. It shimmered like oil on water with all the colours of the rainbow. There and then the fisherman almost fainted when he realised that she was not of his world, but a mermaid from the depths of the ocean.

He had heard stories of mermaids many a time but now, even with one before him, it was still almost beyond belief. Evening after evening he went to the same place to fish and each time she was there. Being a bachelor and living a lonely island existence, it did not take him long to fall in love with the mermaid and imagine the happiness she would bring to his life. But how could he capture her?

The fisherman sought the help of the Old Hag of Rathlin who, the people always said, knew everything.

'I have been waiting for you,' she said with a grin on her face.

'I was fishing,' he said, 'from the shore – up on the north side.'

'Have ye now?'

'I saw a mermaid,' he said breathlessly.

'Have ye now? You're a quare lucky boy.'

'Some people say you know how to catch them.'

'Do they now? You've come till the right place then haven't ye?'

'Can ye tell me? I mean … how to get her.'

'Oh, she'll be easy caught but what will ye do with her when you do?'

'I want her for my wife,' the fisherman blurted out in desperation.

'Do ye now? Well, when you catch her you must take her home straight away. Take the tail off her – it'll come away clean like a stocking. But you must never destroy it, or she will die. Hide it away somewhere, but mind, if ever she finds it she will go back to the ocean, and never more will you see her.'

Well, the fisherman did exactly as he had been told. By a trick he caught the mermaid at low tide. He brought her up the shore and sure enough her tail came away just as the old hag had said. He took her to his tumbledown cabin, such as it was, and hid her tail in the rafters of an outhouse.

Before he knew what had happened the fisherman had a beautiful, long-legged woman of the sea for a wife – and a fine wife she was too. Despite all the fisherman's deceit and selfishness, she was loving and gentle and kind to him. She cooked and kept house for him and as time passed they had two beautiful children – a girl and a boy. Though they were poor, the fisherman and his family seemed to live quite happily and healthily for years. Never was a there a man on Rathlin Island who was more content than he.

One fine morning the fisherman had some matter or other to attend to on the mainland and he set out in a boat that was heading for Ballycastle. It was late that night when he returned but as he approached his home he saw the door lying wide to the wall. There was no light in the doorway nor smoke coming from the chimney. When he went in the fire was dead and the place cold and empty. He came across his children whimpering in a corner. When they told their father all about the strange scaly fish's tail they had found in the rafters, the words of the Old Hag of Rathlin rung in his ears, 'If ever she finds it she will go back to the ocean, and never more will you see her.'

The children wept and wailed for weeks and months and many a night they cried themselves to sleep, for their father could offer them little comfort and no hope of ever seeing their mother again. But every morning in life when the children awoke they were well groomed and their faces clean. There was always food prepared on the table and baskets of fish often left at the door. They grew up poor and always lamented the loss of their mother, but never did those two children want for food in their bellies or a comb pulled through their hair.

For the rest of his days the fisherman felt the terrible pain of grief in his heart, and often he called to the ocean like a man possessed for his sea wife to come back or even just to show herself, but she never did.

THE OLD MAN OF RATHLIN

The curious supernatural being in this story appears more than once in Rathlin folk tales. He may have come about as way of rationalising the loss of young seafaring men who led such hazardous lives. The conditions around the island are notoriously treacherous and it was common enough, even in recent times, for men to be lost in accidents at sea. In the distant past, with its more primitive technology, the attrition rate might have been much higher, especially among the young (and perhaps relatively inexperienced) fishermen. In this dark story there seems to be no way to guard against this force of nature. (R80.29. 19/4/80)

One night many years ago a sail boat came into the island. She was from further along the north coast towards Donegal. On board were a father and his son. They were caught out when a sudden storm blew up and had fought against the winds and the swirling currents until they were almost exhausted. In desperation, they made for a wee inlet on the north end of the island near a place called Courig.

As they got closer they could see a cave just above the shoreline that promised sanctuary from the elements. They managed to run their little boat in and leapt from her on to the shore. Then they tried to haul her up but she was too heavy.

'I'll hold her if you can go and get help,' said the son to his father. The father set off up the steep path to find some island men.

When he came back with help the boat it was sitting well up on the shore high and dry and the son was huddled beside it.

'How did ye ever haul that boat up yerself?' cried the father in amazement, for it was a great miracle of strength.

'I was holding the boat,' answered the son in a breathless, faltering whisper, 'and the wind rose and big swells started coming in. The rope was slipping through my hands and I couldn't hold her, but then an oul fella appeared at my side.

'"I can help you," said he.

'"For God's sake, take the rope," says I.

'"I will," says he, "If you will grant me one small thing of value."

'"Take whatever you want," says I to the oul fella. "Just help me, please."

'So, the old man took the rope and hand over hand he hauled the boat himself. Then, just as he appeared, he vanished into the night.'

Well, the young fellow raised himself to his feet and tried to walk but he was so weak that his father and some of the islandmen had to carry him up the steep path to the nearest cottage. By the dim light of a flickering rush lamp they could see he was still alive but only just. When they began to undo his oilskins, they saw that his great head of black hair had turned pure white. His broad shoulders and well-made arms had wasted away. His skin was wrinkled like an autumn leaf and all his teeth had fallen out.

'What has happened my fine strong son?' cried the father.

The islandmen knew. They told him about the old man who lived in the cave at the bottom of the cliffs.

'Some say he's the Devil himself,' said one.

'He's been there since before the time of our grandfathers and great grandfathers,' said another, 'Waiting for young seafarers who chance to pass his way. He always robs them of the only thing of value they possess – their youth.'

THE VIKING, THE FALCON AND THE OLD MAN OF RATHLIN

This is a much more colourful adaptation of the previous story. The introduction of more characters including enchanted warriors, a desirable chieftain's daughter, a Viking prince as saviour and a magical talking falcon might suggest a more imaginative storyteller. As TC commented himself, the stories 'gained a lot in the telling'. In any case, the whole arc of this tale rises and falls more dramatically. It provides the listeners a little more hope and joy with the classic 'and they all lived happily ever after' ending. Of course, it also explains why Peregrine falcons abound and are revered on the island! (Ref. C79.29. 16/7/79)

It so happened one time that many of the young islandmen were being taken and robbed of their souls. It was said that the thief was a strange creature who appeared as an ancient man the people called the Old Man of Rathlin. He kept the souls of his young victims deep within a cave, the mouth of which was guarded by four warriors whose armour made them all but invincible. It was whispered that the warriors had one mortal weakness, but no one knew what this was or how it might be found. Every father and mother who had lost sons looked to their clan chief for an answer but, powerful as he was, he seemed helpless against the Old Man of Rathlin and his warriors.

The chieftain had a young daughter. She was very beautiful and she attracted the attention of chieftains' sons and princes from all over Erin, Alba and Lochlainn. Any one of them would have gladly taken her for their wife, not least because in so doing, an alliance with the Rathlin chief and a share of his island kingdom would follow. Many had sought approval but the chieftain decreed that only he who could rid the island of the accursed Old Man would be granted his daughter's hand. Few had been able or willing to face the otherworldly warriors or find the weakness in their armour. Any who had tried had never been heard of again.

But then from Lochlainn came an bold and fearless Viking prince who had heard about the chieftain's daughter and all the good that would flow from such a marriage. When the Viking laid eyes on the Rathlin princess he was completely besotted by her and agreed without concern or worry to the terms laid down by her father. He went about the island enquiring from everyone he met how he might defeat the warriors. He spoke to hen wives and holy men but none could tell him what he needed to know. Soon he began to despair of ever finding a way to defeat the warriors who guarded the cave.

As he sat at the edge of the cliff on the north side of the island weighing his choices heavily, he watched a falcon. Suddenly it stooped with great speed, before swooping up to the cliff edge and landing on a tussock of grass right by the Norseman. Its brows were fiercely gathered and its eyes were dark and piercing. Its steely scimitar beak and shiny black talons on long yellow toes glinted like fearsome weapons.

'How beautiful and cruel a creature you are,' said the Viking almost to himself.

'Cruel I may be and yet it is I who am mistreated by the people of this island.'

Well, of course, the Viking was shaken to the very marrow of his bones when he heard the falcon speak.

'Am I dreaming?' he said.

'No,' said the falcon, 'you are not. I am enchanted, as well you might know.'

'Are you under a spell? Have you come to ask for my help?'

'No, my young friend. It is you who are in need of my help if you are to do battle with the warriors who guard the cave of the Old Man of Rathlin.'

'If only I could find the weakness in their armour then I might defeat them.'

Well, to cut a long story short, the enchanted falcon told the Norseman how he could overcome the warriors. In turn, the Viking triumphed. He slew the four warriors and released the souls of all the young men that had been for so long held captive. In so doing he gave the folk of Rathlin their sons back and the island its vitality. What exactly the falcon told the Norseman we shall never know for the prince always kept it a closely guarded secret, but he did tell the people that if not for the falcon they would have suffered under the curse of the Old Man of Rathlin for evermore.

As promised, the Viking was wed to the chieftain's beautiful daughter. Let us hope they reared many children and had a long and happy life together. As for the falcons, well, never again were they hunted or their eggs broken, as the people so often used to do. Instead, the islanders gladly shared the crop of seabirds they too depended on to feed their families. Ever after, it was deemed a great wickedness to even disturb a falcon's eyrie.

Since then, Peregrine falcons have been protected by generations of islanders. Long may those magnificent hunting birds live there in peace, for if ever they should forsake their wild rocky crags it would be a dark day for the youth of Rathlin.

THE VIKING AND THE OLD HAG

For hundreds of years Vikings landed on Rathlin Island. Many are the stories of Norse kings, princes and warriors who came to raid and steal what they could, but then later to trade and some even to find friendship and love. Of them all, this story still has the power to shock and get under the skin of the listener. It is one of those timeless yarns that retains a wisdom and gravity that can yet resonate with a modern-day audience. (R80.16. 17/2/80)

It was a Norse prince who once came to Rathlin and, going around the island, he met with a young woman and instantly he lusted after her. She was the daughter of the chieftain and so the prince had to ask her father's permission to marry her.

'On one condition,' said the chief, 'That you will not take my daughter away to Lochlainn but will live here on Rathlin or within sight of it.'

The Norseman agreed and he soon found a fitting place on the height of Torr Head over on the mainland and within sight of Rathlin. It was a fine stronghold and looked out over the narrowest channel of the Sea of Moyle between Hibernia and Alba, just 12 miles away. But the fort was held by another chieftain and the Norseman did not have the men and arms to take it by force.

'I will return to my homeland, and within seven years and a day I will bring back warriors enough to take the fort on Torr Head. Then I will marry your daughter,' said the Viking.

The Rathlin chief agreed. His daughter bid farewell to her suitor and the time passed.

As the years went by, other men came to seek the hand of the Rathlin princess. The old chieftain soon became impatient and, giving no more thought to the Norseman, he married his daughter off to another chieftain's son. The young couple set up hearth and home in a castle on the island they call Kilpatrick and children soon followed.

But then one morning sails appeared on the horizon. It was the Viking prince returned. This time he had longboats and men enough to take the stronghold on Torr Head. After a bloody battle he installed himself as chieftain and went over to Rathlin to claim his bride.

'You are too late,' said the Rathlin chief, 'My daughter has been wed to another.'

In his fury the Norseman drew his sword and slew the old chieftain there and then. With his men he attacked Castle Kilpatrick. The battle was savage and bloody, but in the end the Vikings put everyone to the sword – the Rathlin princess, her husband and, such was the Viking prince's anger and bitterness, even their small children.

When all the bloodletting was over many lay dead and injured. The Viking prince had almost lost his right arm to the sword of a Rathlin warrior. His glory days were over. He would have to return to Lochlainn a beaten man, for a Viking warrior not killed in battle and unable to fight more was no better than a slave of the land. The Gods would not welcome him as a hero into Valhalla. But an islander told his men of an old hag who was possessed of great powers. They took their leader to the woman in the hope that she could help him.

'I can give you back the power of your arm,' she told the Norseman.

'Save my arm and I will give you anything,' he said.

'Very well,' said she, 'and in time I will return to collect my reward.'

'Anything you ask, if it is in my power to give it will be yours,' he promised.

The old hag was fit to heal the Norseman's wounds and give him back the power of his arm. Soon he was able to hold a sword again and regained his standing as captain of his men. He led them on raids all around the north coast and great were the riches they gained. Eventually the Norseman came back to settle on Rathlin and found a local woman to be his wife.

Not long afterwards she gave birth to a baby son. When the Norseman was told the child was well and healthy he was filled with joy and contentment. That night there was great feasting and celebrations to wet the baby's head. As the festivities were going on, a visitor came to the Norseman's stronghold. It was the old hag who had given him back his arm.

'Come in and you are welcome,' said the Norseman to the old woman.

'I thank you,' she said.

'This is she who gave me back my arm,' he declared to all assembled at the feast. To a man the warriors and guests cheered and raised their cups in praise.

'Indeed, I was,' she said, 'and now I have come to collect my reward.'

'Ask anything,' said the Norseman, 'and if it is in my power to give I will happily – for I gave my word, and it shall not be broken.'

'I am glad to hear it,' said the woman, 'and now if you please sir, I will have your newborn son.'

A deathly silence fell over the hall as the old woman's words sank in.

'My son?' But you cannot take my son,' cried the Norseman.

'Would you break your word sir?' asked the old woman fiercely, 'You who have slaughtered men, women and children for such a slight?'

The Norseman made no answer. Broken-hearted as he and his poor wife were, he could not go back on his word and the old hag left with their son wrapped in swaddling.

A year and a day passed, and the Norseman's wife gave birth to another son. The child was healthy, and his parents were overjoyed. Some of the pain and suffering they had endured at the loss of their first born seemed to ease a little.

A great feast was arranged. As the celebrations were in full sway and the men were raising their cups and greasing their innards with roast boar and venison and salmon, again the old hag came knocking on the door. Again, she reminded the Norseman of the promise he had made to her. And once again, she demanded his newborn son. It was almost more suffering than the Norseman could bear. But his word could not be broken, and the old woman left with the child wrapped in swaddling.

He and his wife were utterly bereft, but a year and a day passed, and she gave birth to another baby boy. There was great sadness through-out the household, however. The Norseman never even enquired as to the child's wellbeing for he knew in his heart of hearts the old hag would return. But as the day wore on he became more and more defiant. He ordered a feast to be arranged. Just as before, the old hag appeared and made her demand.

'I will have your newborn son,' she said.

'No!' cried the Norseman boldly. 'You will not have my son. Enough is enough.'

The old hag laughed at this and said, 'I knew you would not hold to your word. Keep your child. He will bring you no joy for he will never fight in battle, nor will your Gods welcome him or you into Valhalla.'

With that the old hag left, and the Norseman ran to his wife's side to tell her the news. She was nursing their child and as she did her tears fell on his little head.

'Fear not,' said the Norseman, 'All will be well.'

But as he spoke, his wife unwrapped the swaddling to reveal that their baby son had only one little arm.

The tormented Norseman ran from that chamber shouting and screaming that he was a man cursed. In his madness, he threw himself over the walls of the castle on to the rocks far below and so ended his own tortured life.

Some say that once he realised his terrible sins, so long overdue, were to be paid for by his innocent son, he could no longer live with himself. We will never know what went through the Viking's mind, but perhaps men who live by the sword can only go on living if they never have to look at themselves or peer into their own souls.

THE THREE STONES

There are many folk tales of seafarers and travellers finding themselves in Norway and encountering old men who claim to have detailed knowledge of a particular townland or farm on Rathlin or on the mainland. The protagonist then reveals that their ancestors were displaced when the Vikings were driven out of Ireland following their defeat at the Battle of Clontarf in 1214. This is a charming variation of that narrative with a positive if not exactly happy ending. (R80.16 17/2/80)

It is a good many years ago that a young Rathlin man took itchy feet and went, like so many before him, travelling around the world as a mariner. He sailed on different boats here and there but eventually ended up in Norway.

Paid off from his ship and with no way home, he stayed there for a while working on fishing boats around the fjords. All the knowledge he had picked up from being born and bred on Rathlin as a fisherman came in very useful. As time went by he moved from place to place, never having anywhere to stay permanently, but one day he met a young woman.

'You can come and stay with my family,' she said after she heard his story. 'You can help us with the fishing until the summer and then maybe find a ship to take you back home.'

The young Rathlin man accepted her generosity and she took him home to meet her family.

'Where is it you hail from?' asked the young woman's grandfather one evening.

'A wee island called Rathlin,' answered the young fellow, 'You have likely never heard tell of it.'

'I know Rathlin well,' said the old man. 'What part of the island are you from?'

'I'm from down the lower end – near a place they call Ushet Lough.'

'Ah, I know Ushet,' said the old man.

'Oh! Have you been to Rathlin before?' asked the young fellow, quite surprised.

'No, but I have people belonging to me there,' said the old man with a sigh.

Well, the young fellow thought this was very strange, but he asked no more questions for he made up his mind the old Norwegian must be starting to dote.

All through the winter and spring the young fellow stayed with the family and worked at the fishing. They looked after him well, but by the summertime he had found a boat that was sailing south and would eventually get him home to Rathlin.

'I will be leaving soon,' he said to the family. 'I am indebted to you for your kindness. I would like to do something for you in return if I can.'

'You can do something for me,' said the old grandfather.

'If it is within my gift I will,' said the young fellow earnestly.

'There are three large stones lying on the ground near to Ushet,' said the grandfather with tears in his eyes. 'Do you know them?'

'I know the stones you speak of well,' said the young fellow.

'Good. When you get home I want you to bury them for me.'

'Bury them! But why?'

'They are three of my kinfolk. They fell in battle a thousand years ago and their comrades had not the time to lay them to rest. They were turned to stone with a vow that one day someone would return to bury them. Do this for me and your debt of gratitude will be paid in full.'

When he eventually got back home to Rathlin the first thing the young fellow did was to dig a grave. He laid the three stones side by side where they had fallen all those years before, and he covered them over with earth. And there they lie under the Rathlin sod to this day undisturbed by wind or weather. A lump of limestone rises out of the ground to mark their eternal resting place.

The old folk on the island always said it was a good and decent thing that the young fellow did. No one likes to think of kinfolk not laid to rest – however far away they are, or however many years have passed.

THE FAERIE MIDWIFE

Storytellers from almost every corner of Ireland, Scotland and the north of England claim a version of this folk tale as theirs. The truth is that across these islands there are numerous variants. Present in this rendering, however, are a few details that are quite unique to Rathlin Island. I could not resist the temptation to portray this as the original version and who knows, it may well be! (C79.29. 16/7/79)

At one time there lived in every townland and parish of the country a henwife or wise woman. They were healers and herbalists, midwives and embalmers and, of course, on Rathlin there was just such a woman. She lived at the low end of the island and like all her kind she was seldom idle.

One night, when the wind was blowing a full gale and the rain coming sideways in off the ocean, this woman went to her bed hoping to get some rest in spite of the storm. But she wasn't long in the blankets before she heard a knock at the door. When she looked out she could just see by the faint light from her own window what looked like a coach and team of four horses standing on the road. The woman thought this very strange for she knew of no one on the island who possessed or needed such a fine team – not even Gage, the landlord. Then the woman heard a voice.

'Come right away missus. There's a woman in the throes of labour and in great need of your services.'

Well, she thought she could see a small figure in the darkness, but she did not recognise the strange voice. Besides, she knew every blessed sinner on the island and could think of no one near their time. Nevertheless, she packed a bag with all the things she might need. Wrapping a shawl around her head, she went out into the night, safe in the knowledge that no harm had ever come to one of her profession.

Helped by a wee man dressed in black, she stepped up into the coach and it took off like lightning. It hadn't gone far when it left the road. Away over the bog they went, through heather and rushes where a man could barely walk never mind horses gallop. By now the midwife was beginning to regret leaving her wee cabin but then the carriage began to slow. When she looked out the window she recognised the place, for they were coming up to the back of a hill called Brockley near the other end of the island. As they came closer, the hill suddenly opened and the carriage was swallowed up.

Inside the hill the midwife stepped down from the carriage. Her jaw almost fell to the ground for she had never seen the likes. The walls were all decorated with butterflies' wings that shimmered by the light of a thousand little flaming torches. There were great banqueting tables ladened with platters of roast meats and loaves of bread. There were wee folk playing music and dancing and drinking from goblets of gold and silver, and not one took any notice of the midwife.

The wee man in black led her away to a chamber where lay a tiny wee woman in the latter distressing throes of labour. The midwife went to work immediately. God only knows how long she toiled for she lost track of time completely, but eventually the little woman gave birth to a healthy wee baby boy the size of a leveret.

When everything was done and the child at his mother's little breast, the midwife was quietly led back out to where she had arrived. It was only then she began to recognise people she had known from the island – young boys and girls who had disappeared over the years. She tried to speak to some of them but not one paid her any heed.

Then the wee folk began to come around her very mannerly and bid her welcome.

'Here, have something to eat,' said one.

'Take a drink for you must be thirsty,' said another.

And right enough, the midwife had been so busy with the delivery of the baby she had no time to think of food or drink. Now that it was mentioned to her, she felt the stabs of hunger and a raging thirst was on her. Thinking there was no harm in it, she accepted the wee folk's kindness. But as she waited to be served, a young girl who was sitting by a fire nursing a baby began to sing a strange lullaby.

Let not a scrap of faerie food,
E'r pass your lips for if it should,
Never more will you see daylight.
Be sure and go straight home the night.

Over and over the young girl lilted the warning and lucky it was for the midwife that she did, for slowly it began to dawn on her the peril she was in. If she were to let a single drop of drink or a morsel of faerie food pass her lips she would never be able to leave the faerie world – not of her own free will anyway.

The midwife gathered her belongings and demanded to be taken home straight away.

'Ugh, stay for just one night,' the faerie folk pleaded, but the midwife steadfastly refused. So, home she was taken in the same carriage. It was still dark when she arrived, and her fire was glowing red as she had left it and the candle burning in the window.

For days the midwife fretted. Greatly troubled in her mind, she eventually went to Gage. She told her landlord everything that she had seen and heard that night the faerie folk came for her. He listened to her story intently, only interrupting to clarify some small detail here and there. Afterwards, he thought deeply for a long time before he spoke to her.

'I must warn you,' he said, 'if ever you breathe this to another living soul I will have you evicted and banished from this island forever.'

Why Gage took the position he did God only knows. He must have had his reasons. As for the midwife, plainly she defied her master for her story spread like wildfire and, even yet, it is told from County Antrim to County Cork. If Gage carried out his threats of eviction against the poor woman no one now remembers. Let us hope that he did not.

THE HUNTING PARTY
AND THE HARE

I first heard a version of this story told by a Welsh storyteller. It was the same in almost every respect, except with regard to details of location. It is a great example of how easily folk tales travel – almost as easily as storytellers! In this version the poor tenant, through magical means, gets the better of their overbearing landlord and his rich guests. Better still, they do so without him knowing a thing about it, thereby striking a blow for the downtrodden islanders. It is a delightful twist on this type of 'triumphant underdog' story. (C79.29. 16/7/79)

It happened one year that the landlord brought some of his wealthy and influential friends over from the mainland. They brought with them fowling pieces to shoot the wild ducks and geese and hounds to course the hares, for game was as plentiful on the island then as it is now. The hunting party were gabbling away like excited children, and the hounds were yelping and barking as they made their way to the Upper End. They met a young island boy coming down the track and, eager to ensure good sport for his friends, Gage spoke to the child.

'Good morning,' said he to the wee fellow. 'Are there many hares about this part of the island do you know?'

'Not so many sir, but there's one or two where you're going.'

'Is there now? Do think you could find out where I might rise one on my way back. I would pay a good ghillie half a crown,' said Gage, turning the silver coin in his fingers.

Well, half a crown was a small fortune in those far-off days and the wee boy's eyes nearly popped out on his cheeks. He ran down home to his grandmother and told her what Gage had said. The old woman was baking at bread, but she listened intently. When the wee boy finished she cleaned the flour from her hands and bent down to look into his eyes.

'Go you up to the hill and wait for them fine gentlemen to come back down from the Upper End. When you see them tell Gage that there's a fine big hare lying in below yon whin bush at the side of the road.'

In his eagerness the wee fellow ran out the door like lightning. Up to the hill he went and waited for the hunting party to come back along the road. He couldn't keep himself still with excitement and had to pee more than once, but eventually he saw the heads of the men coming bobbing along over the gorse bushes.

'Mr Gage. Mr Gage, there's a big fine hare lying in below that there whin bush,' said the wee fellow, and he pointed to the big, jagged mound of gorse covered with yellow blossom at the side of the track.

Well, the men surrounded the place and as one they slipped the collars from their straining hounds. The hare flew out by them like the wind. It ran down the hill with the dogs close behind. But the hare jinked this way and that and the hounds were not as familiar with the rough ground. Down behind the church the hare raced and then it made a bee's line for the grandmother's house. The hounds followed and coming panting and shouting behind were the men, burdened as they were by their big cumbersome boots and heavy fowling pieces.

The hare ran straight into the grandmother's house and the door slammed shut behind it. When the men arrived breathless a few minutes later, the hounds were yelping and whining around the door.

'Missus are you there?' called Gage. 'Is there anyone home?'

Gage went forward and lifted the latch on the door. Men and hounds all landed into the tiny cabin.

'How dare you Mr Gage,' said the woman of the house breathlessly, her face as flushed and red as a beetroot. 'Landlord ye may be but I pay my rent and surely to God I'm entitled to some privacy.'

'My apologies Ma'am,' said Gage, 'but have you seen a hare?'

'I've seen no hare the day, only a shower of ill-mannered gulls and gowling beagles. Now if you wouldn't mind ...'

Well, the men backed out of the little cabin and, disgruntled as they were, repaired to the Manor House for hot brandies, port wine and other refreshments. When they had gone the grandmother looked over at her wee grandson standing there beaming from ear to ear at the door.

'Well?' she said. 'Did ye get the half a crown son?'

'I did,' said the wee fellow as he flipped the silver coin through the air.

'Good boy,' she said laughing, 'but you might have told me about them hounds.'

'Aye, granny, I'm sorry about that, I just forgot but by jeepers you gave them a quare run for their money,' he said bursting with pride.

That night as the wee fellow slept by the fire, his grandmother dabbed iodine on to a few wee red scratches where the briars had pulled at her skin. In the Manor House, Gage and his hunting party drank their fill of brandy punch. They talked long into the wee hours and wondered to God how that hare had ever got away from them.

A LUCKY ESCAPE

Often entitled the Rathlin Faerie Story, I have heard versions of this folk tale told by local storytellers whose source was TC. Other islanders told the tale, and it also appears in a publication produced by the Causeway Coast Museum Service, Lore of the Land, *2019. Interestingly, I have also heard a variant from Cornwall where the stolen child is so filthy because of his neglectful mother that the faeries cannot rid him of all earthly traces. (C79.29. 16/7/79)*

It's many years ago now that a young boy – I won't name him, for his descendants live on the island yet – went missing. It was a lovely clear blue morning in early September. The dew was heavy on the grass and the whin bushes were swathed in a gauze of spider webs. After his breakfast the wee fellow's mother sent him out blackberry picking with a promise to stew the berries and an apple for his supper.

'Don't be straying too far now,' she said, 'and don't be gorbing on them blackberries or you'll make yourself be sick.'

By evening time, the mother was near out of her mind with worry, for her wee son hadn't come home. The neighbours gathered in around the house for news and to comfort the woman. The men went out searching the roads and the bogs and along the clifftops and beaches. They dragged wells and lakes. Candles were lit and prayers said. Two days and three nights they searched for him, but neither hide nor hair of the wee fellow could they find.

At the finish up, the men said he must have fallen over a cliff and been swept away by the tide. Maybe his wee body would be washed ashore in good time, they said. The family's home became a wake house as his poor parents grieved for their loss.

Early on the third morning the wee fellow wandered in through the door. He was shining like a new pin, for he was as well groomed as if he was going to make his first Communion. He was neither hungered nor hurt.

'Where in the name of God Almighty have ye been?' asked his mother through her tears and disbelief.

'I was took by the faeries,' the wee fellow blurted out excitedly, 'I was just gathering blackberries up behind the hill when I heard laughing and I turned round and saw wee children running and hiding down in the hollow. I only went down to see Ma, but it wasn't children at all. It was wee folk. They took my clothes, and they scrubbed and scrubbed and scrubbed me with soap till my skin was burning. They gave me new britches and a shirt, but I wouldn't put them on. They tried to get me to eat but I was bawling and crying and kept telling them I wanted to go home.'

'And then what happened?' said his mother.

'Nothing. They just let me go.'

Everyone who heard the story agreed that the wee folk had been trying to steal the child, as they often did. The faeries had taken his clothes away and scrubbed him to get rid of every earthly trace, as they always did. But why they had let him go in the end no one could imagine.

But wasn't the mother glad to have her wee son home again and him as healthy as a trout. She set him up to the table and a big bowl of porridge and as he shovelled the oats into his mouth he remarked quite innocently, 'My thumb's sore Ma.'

'Let me see son,' said his mother tenderly.

And right enough, the wee fellow's thumb was all red and inflamed. Clean as it was, which was rare, the mother took his wee thumb into her mouth. She could feel the heat in it and with her tongue felt something sharp sticking out from under his thumbnail.

'It's a jag you have under your nail,' she said, her eyes squinting by the light of the window. With a needle that she retrieved from her apron, and much to the wee fellow's displeasure, she dug out a tiny briar thorn the size of a midge's leg.

'That's what saved you son,' she said. 'Only for that tiny wee thorn, the faeries would have kept ye. Isn't it a blessing to God they never found it.'

It was indeed a lucky escape. But for that one small earthly trace that tethered him to the human world, the child would likely never have been seen again – not this side of the veil anyway.

THE FISHERMAN AND THE CAT

There are many anecdotes in the TC archive relating to Old Nick – the Devil! He appears as a stranger dressed in black at late-night card schools or as a big black dog with burning red eyes along dark winter roads to drunkards staggering home. In these sketches he seems always to be an uninvited visitor to where some wickedness or impiety, according to religious morals, is afoot. Rathlin folk terrified each other with stories of these appearances and strange happenings for generations. The following story has similarities to other folk tales involving feline apparitions, where the creature is sometimes portrayed as a witch rather than a devil. (C79.29. 16/7/79)

There was once a man who was coming back from the east side of the island after a day's fishing. It was November and though it was not very late, only for the flickering lights from cabin windows and a few stars here and there it was pitch dark. The man was making his way home to Ballyconaghan carrying two or three strings of mackerel and wee codlings with about a dozen on each.

As he was going up Tromore Hill he suddenly became aware of a big black cat standing on the track in front of him. It was no farm mouser out on the prowl of an evening. It was four or maybe five times the size of an ordinary cat and its green eyes fixed the fisherman so menacingly he began to fear for his life. Then the idea came to him to distract the creature with a fish. He pulled one off the string and threw it to the side of the track. The cat went to the fish and began to eat. The man slipped by and, breathing heavily now, he quickened his pace.

On up the hill the fisherman went but then suddenly the cat appeared again – standing there in the track staring at him. Again, he threw down a fish and just as before the cat went towards it and the man slipped by. Over and over and over again this happened until the man was nearing his homeplace, but by now he had no fish left. Seeing his own cabin up ahead, he made a run for it and tried to get past the cat, but it pounced on his back.

The screeches and wails of that cat would have wakened the dead. All the man could do was curl up and protect himself as best he could. He felt the beast's claws tear through his heavy oilskins and it's needle-sharp teeth sink into his flesh. The man called out for his wife and to God for help and then suddenly, just as quickly as the attack began, it ceased. The creature disappeared into the darkness and the night became deathly quiet.

The fisherman lay there for a long time in the cold, shivering with fear, waiting for the beast to return and finish him off, but it never did. Eventually, he dragged himself to his feet and staggered on home. By the light of a candle, he tried to take his clothes off, but he was too weak and collapsed to the floor. The commotion brought his wife from her bed.

'What time do you call this to be staggering home and not a fish or feather. Were ye in that dirty oul pub or some shabeen drinking poitín? You reek like the hobs of hell.'

And right enough, her husband's clothes bore a stench like rotten eggs that could not be explained otherwise. As she helped him take off his torn garments she threw them out the door. She was shaken to find so many gashes and cuts all over her husband's body – some of them right to the bone.

'Dear God, did ye fall over a cliff or were ye pulled through a thorn hedge backwards?'

The woman slowly unwound as she vented her anger, and concern and pity took over. She treated her husband's wounds – packing the worst and stitching some up as best she could.

For days the man was at death's door, and the priest was sent for. Eventually he came around, but in spite of every question that was asked of him, he refused to tell a soul what had happened. Of course, the neighbours began to make up their own stories. They said he must have been drunk and fallen over a cliff, as his wife suspected. They said he was too ashamed to tell the truth or too drunk to remember. They said he was very lucky to be alive and they were right about that.

Very slowly the fisherman recovered. After weeks in bed, he eventually raised himself up and like a child took his first steps. His appetite and his strength began to return but still he refused to tell his wife what had happened to him. It was months before he could go outside again and never in the dark.

Even as the fisherman recovered and was feeling stronger in himself, not a decent night's sleep could he get. His wife was so worried she sent for the priest again and so persistent was he that the fisherman slowly told him everything that had happened.

'Were you drunk man – now tell me the truth?' said the priest.

'I was not Father.'

'Well then, why did you not tell anyone about this until now?'

'Father, I was attacked by a devil out of hell!' said the fisherman grimly, 'Maybe Oul Nick himself. I had a great fear on me that I would die if I told another living soul.'

Well, there was more conversation between the two men but eventually the priest said a few prayers and blessed the fisherman.

'You'll be grand now,' he said. 'So put all thoughts of this from your head.'

The priest bid the fisherman and his wife farewell and left, but the fisherman could not banish the haunting visions from his mind nor the fear of death that was upon him. All that day he sat in his chair and stared into the fire. He hardly spoke two words. When his wife got up the next morning he was still sitting in the chair by the fire – but he was as dead as a stone!

And that's a true story, for it was the priest himself who told it.

A PRIEST'S CURSE

There are three main types of curses that often appear in Irish folk tales: a saint's, a widow's and a priest's. The following are two examples of the latter and they are characteristic of the downtrodden priest acting against his or the people's oppressor, usually with divine assistance, though this is not entirely obvious in the first short story. Here the victims of the clergyman's ire seem rather innocent. They are caught between a rock and a hard place and in this interpretation the priest appears as a something of bully. In the second, the clergyman is little better but equally powerful. (C79.29. 16/7/79 & R80.29. 19/4/80)

There was once a priest who was refused passage to Rathlin by boatmen employed by the landlord.

'I'm sorry Father, we cannot take ye,' said one of the boatmen, 'Mr Gage would have our lives.'

'Gage be damned, take me over to Rathlin or you'll have me to deal with!' bellowed the priest.

'Will you feed our weans when Gage evicts us Father?' asked the boatman.

As the little boat sailed out of Ballycastle, the clergyman was left on the pier. He was raging mad, but on the peril of their livelihoods, the ferrymen had been instructed by their employer not to carry Catholic clergymen to the island. In his fury the priest cursed the poor but defiant boatmen who sailed without him.

'Before this day is out you will be damned glad of me,' he cried after them.

That evening as the men returned to the mainland, their little boat struck a rock off Rue Point. All were lost. Their tragic deaths were put down to the clergyman's curse! His regret or otherwise was not recorded.

Many years later the wife of Gage met the island priest along the road – which was only wide enough to let one horse by at a time. The islanders always deferred to the Gages when they met on the road and stepped aside to let their landlord or landlady by. The priest, however, refused to yield.

'I am going to attend a dying man. Step aside ma'am,' said the priest.

'I will not,' said Mrs Gage, 'Tis you who should step aside.'

And so, the ructions started, but the priest gave as good as he got. Eventually he said, 'I have not the time to argue with you Mrs Gage, but you will be here when I return.'

He steered his horse out around the flaming Mrs Gage and went to give his dying parishioner the last rights.

The priest was detained much longer than he expected and was coming back along the road very late. When he reached the place where he had clashed with Mrs Gage, there she was still standing as he had left her, unable to move. Whether the priest meant to curse the lady of Manor House to teach her a lesson or some greater power intervened on his behalf, no one knows, but Mrs Gage was certainly a chastened woman – for a while anyway.

THE MAN WHO
TALKED TO THE WIND

This story tells of a young fisherman not being cursed so much as warned very sternly and gravely by a venerated elder. Unheeding of the insight offered him, the fisherman, it might be said, suffers a much more profound consequence than mere death. It is a fine example, I think, of the type of folk tale that often develops among people living at the mercy of their raw environment, who endeavour to make sense of the natural forces prevailing and weave their perceived wisdom into it. (C79.29. 16/7/79)

It used to be well known that there was a man on Rathlin who talked to the wind. All the other fishermen on the island went to him for advice before they would set sail. He was always right, and everyone had faith in him.

As time passed fishermen came from the north, south, east and west to fish around Rathlin. They heard about the man who talked to the wind. They always came to seek his advice and he would always tell them what mood the wind was in and how it might behave. He was never wrong, and the fishermen trusted him completely. More and more fishermen came in bigger and bigger currachs. They would stay on Rathlin, sleeping in caves at night, and fish around the coast for a few days at a time. Always they took the advice of the man who talked to the wind.

Then one year a young fisherman came across the Sea of Moyle in a big newly built currach. He needed help with his fishing lines and so asked another young Rathlin fellow to give him a hand. One day, as they were getting their gear ready to set out from the island, the man who talked to the wind came along.

'There's going to be a gale blowing up out of the east. You'd be wiser not to venture out the day,' he said.

The young man from across the sea looked out at the water. It was as calm as a pond.

'I doubt there'll be any wind today,' he said.

'I tell ye,' said the man who talked to the wind, 'there's a gale coming.'

'Well, I'm going to chance it anyway for I don't believe in all your old gibberish.'

The man who talked to the wind was beside himself with rage for no one had ever questioned his wisdom before.

'You're a fool,' he said. 'If ye go against my advice you'll rue the day, for never again will you set foot on dry land.'

'Ah well, we'll see,' said the young stranger.

When he heard this the young Rathlin fellow, wise man that he was, lifted his gear and went away home, leaving his new crewmate to go to sea alone.

The wind rose that evening and it blew a gale out of the east for three days and nights. Then it swung round and began to blow out of the west. It has been doing that ever since and as the old fishermen of Rathlin always say, 'The east is never in debt to the west'. And neither it is, for whenever there is an easterly gale, sooner or later it always shifts and blows just as hard and as long from out of the west.

Just as the man who talked to the wind foretold, the foolish young fisherman never set foot on dry land again. To this day he is drifting back and forth on the Sea of Moyle – eternally blown away by the east wind and then wearily back again by the western gales.

FROM BEYOND THE SENSES

Here are combined four slightly different anecdotes of what might be considered examples of extrasensory perception or supernatural intervention. They reflect only a small number of the various mysterious and eerie episodes described by TC, who personally experienced more than one (see introduction). Of course, these kinds of otherworldly anecdotes are myriad throughout Ireland and are likely just part of the wider human experience. They are no less interesting for all that. (C79.29. 16/7/79 & C79.32. 18/7/79)

Sometimes, our sight, hearing, touch, taste and smell can play little tricks on us. It's no wonder then that we shy away from anything that seems to come to us from beyond our senses. And yet it used to happen on Rathlin all the time. Take the strange tale of a young island boy who was happily going to school one morning with his friend. As they passed by a wee lough, of which there are many on Rathlin, he looked up and saw a strange priest walking along the far bank.

'Look,' he said to his friend, 'who's that priest over there?'

'Where? I can't see a thing,' replied his friend scanning the horizon.

'There on the far side of the water.'

'Ah, you're pullin' me leg.'

'I am not – look, there he is walking along the shore there.'

The whole way down the road the young boy saw the priest, who was walking along in the same direction but always on the far side of the water or a wall, or a field length away. Eventually the clergyman disappeared, but as the two boys were coming round the back of the chapel to go on down to school the same priest appeared again. Just as before, his friend saw nothing. This frightened the life out of the young boy and so upset was he about it all that the school master sent him home for the day.

He wasn't home half an hour when a telegram arrived to inform his mother that her cousin, who was a priest in Glasgow and had left the island years before, had died quite suddenly. Could it have been that the young boy was sensitive to the looming death or was he somehow witnessing the priest's spirit returning home? We will never know.

Of course, shadows of doom and disaster appear in many strange forms – some with more helpful and bewildering outcomes than others.

There were two good neighbours on Rathlin one time, and the older man had a mare that was in foal. Knowing that he was unwell, the younger neighbour offered to help when the time came. As the weeks went by, the older neighbour's health declined, and he became so ill that everyone was waiting on him to die.

With all that was going on, the younger neighbour forgot about the mare. One evening he was down at the shore trying to get a few pollack for the table. As he fished away he heard a cry and looked up the path behind him. There he saw his old neighbour and he thought, 'By God he's back on his feet.' It was then he remembered about the mare, and he thought, 'Damn, she must be about to foal, and he's come all this way to get me.'

'I'm coming now,' he shouted up and pulled in his lines.

The younger man hurried back to where his neighbour had the mare stabled but could not catch up with him. When he got there the mare was already started but her owner was nowhere to be seen. The young man rolled up his sleeves and tended the animal. She gave birth to a fine strong foal and when it was on its feet the young man went to tell his neighbour the good news.

When he reached the house all the old man's family and friends had gathered, and the priest was there. Everyone was solemn and sad. The young neighbour was dumbfounded to hear that the old man had died just a short time earlier. He had never left what was in fact his death bed.

Years before this, there was a hard-working young farmer who kept a few sheep. One day he was shearing his stock at a place called Altaweel. There was good grazing down there below the cliffs. He had about two dozen sheep in a makeshift pen and was about halfway through them when he heard his mother calling, as she often did, from the clifftop up above.

'Come up – you're needed for a run to Ballycastle,' came the familiar voice.

Like most island men, the young fellow had more than one job. As well as working at a bit of farming he kept a boat, which he used to ferry people back and forward to the mainland. So, he let go the sheep, gathered up all the wool and threw it on to his back. Up he went to the house thinking he would finish the sheep the following day.

'Who's looking me to go to Ballycastle?' he said to his mother when he got back.

'Eh?' she said over her shoulder as she worked away. 'What are ye talking about?'

'Sure you're only after shouting on me,' he said impatiently.

'I am not,' said she. 'I haven't left the house this morning.'

Well, wondering what sort of trick had been played on him, the young farmer decided to stay and have a drop of tae with his mother and some of the soda bread she had just lifted off the griddle.

As he walked back to where he had been working he was lamenting the time that had been wasted, but when he got to Altaweel he could hardly believe his eyes. The huge cliff that overhung where the sheep pen had been was gone. It had given way and hundreds of tons of rock had fallen right where the young farmer had been just a short time before.

'You may say a prayer and thank your guardian angel for someone was looking after you this day,' was all his mother said to him.

For centuries untold, some ancient Gaelic families like the O'Haras, the O'Neills, the O'Cahans and the McDonnells have relied on the clan banshee – bean sí – to herald the death of one of their own. But on Rathlin there was a well-known family, some of whom are on the island yet, who had the death of one of their members foreshadowed by the sighting of a strange ghostly boat. Sometimes it was rowed by six oarsmen, sometimes it had a dark sail raised.

Many people swore to have seen it, and it's not that many years ago that there were two men working in the forestry woods at the far end of the island. They were waiting on their wages coming from the mainland when they saw a sail heading out from Church Bay. Thinking it must have been the mailboat that had braved the stormy weather, they made their way down to the harbour to collect their pay packets. By the time they got to the quay there was no sign of the boat.

'Was that the mailboat just sailed out?' one asked the men working at the harbour.

'Mailboat?' There's no boat came in the day. Sure, it's far too rough,' came the answer.

Within a day or two, a member of this family had died. The sighting of the boat by the two forestry men was thought to have been an omen of the death. Others said it was nothing more than happenstance. But the old folk always accepted that there were many things beyond the understanding of ordinary mortals.

MASSACRE ON RATHLIN

The Earl of Essex, Walter Devereux, accompanied by, among others, an ambitious young captain by the name of Francis Drake – later to be knighted by Queen Elizabeth I of England – committed one of the most infamous atrocities ever visited on the people of Rathlin. It was in 1575 that an overwhelming force of English soldiers murdered six hundred men, women and children, of whom only two hundred were armed defenders. They had lain down their weapons after being led to believe that terms were agreed allowing them safe passage to Scotland. It was a lie. Sorley Boy McDonnell's entire family perished in the massacre as he watched helpless from the Antrim shore. Essex later boasted that Sorley Boy was 'like to run mad from sorrow'. The following story is of a later massacre and contains a morsel of hope in the midst of darkness. (C79.29. 16/7/79 & C79.32. 18/7/79)

Over the sixty odd years that followed the terrible slaughter of 1575 on Rathlin, the McDonnell clan repopulated the island, only to be massacred again in 1642, this time by their bitter enemies Clan Campbell. On the orders of Archibald, 8th Earl of Argyll, Rathlin was raided by sixteen hundred covenanter troops led by Sir Duncan Campbell, 6th Lord of Auckenbreck. His instructions were to kill as many of the Catholic McDonnells as he could. The McDonnell force, which numbered fewer than three hundred armed men, did not stand a chance.

The two clans met in a hollow at the centre of the island that came to be known as Lag-na-vis-ta-vor from the old Irish, Log an Chatha Mhóir (Hollow of the Great Battle). It was, in truth, more of a slaughter than a battle. From a hill overlooking the gory field the women watched and keened as their menfolk were cut down like corn. Ever after it was known as Crock na Screedlin (the Hill of Screaming).

When the Campbells had finished off the last of the McDonnell fighting men they turned their bloodlust on the women and children. Scores were stripped naked and either put to the sword or thrown, still alive, over the cliffs. At one steep gully still called Sliocht na Cailleach (Passage of the Hag), dozens of screaming women were tossed down on to the rocks below. One, who had watched in horror as her friends and neighbours were put to death in such cruel fashion, began to take her garments off at the clifftop.

'If you were anything like a gentleman,' she said bitterly to the Campbell soldier. 'You'd turn your back while I undress.'

As the young man did so she grabbed him from behind and threw herself over the edge, taking him with her. He was killed instantly, but somehow or another the woman fell on the bodies of those who had gone before her and by some miracle survived. Winded and in agony, she lay there as if dead but was later rescued by a passing boat manned by McDonnells and taken to Islay. Battered and bruised, the poor woman recovered from her many bodily injuries, but her heart remained broken in two. God only knows what torment and grief she suffered.

Years later the woman returned to Rathlin with a deep yearning to see her home down by Bishop Lough once more. As she approached the old farmstead she expected to see it in ruins, but smoke rose straight up from the chimney. The thatch was in good order and the little field was ploughed and well tended. She sighed wearily, for it had been where she was most content with her husband and the children running happy and free.

She supposed someone had taken over the place and rebuilt the home for themselves. She was right, of course, but as she watched from afar she thought she recognised the bearing of the young man drawing water from the well. The way he moved and stopped to look around him was all so familiar. But how could it be so? Suddenly she was filled with a great urge to find out.

She made her way down to the cabin and though she had not seen him for many years she soon recognised her young son, for he was the spitting image of his long-dead father. When the Campbells came he had been caught out and, clever boy that he was, he hid himself in a midden. The pillaging soldiers had not thought to search a pile of steaming animal dung. When the massacre was over he survived all alone and sought sanctuary in the only place he felt safe – his own home.

There were one or two other survivors, but it might have been better for them if they had perished with the rest. Another young boy escaped by hiding in a cave for months and living off shellfish and the fresh water that dripped down through the rocks. It was said he could only squawk like a gull after his long trial. At least one poor woman was stolen away by a Campbell soldier who took a passing fancy to her. Her fate was not recorded.

The story of the returning woman who found her son is the only faint glimmer of light and hope in this darkest of island chapters. But isn't it heart-warming to think that this, at least, might just have had a happy ending?

THE WOMAN WHO
COULD RISE THE WIND

Not counting mainland Ireland, the island with which Rathlin seems most closely connected is Islay. Wild and windswept and just 20 miles to the north, it is known as the Queen of the Hebrides. Because of their unique geography and long history, the stormy sea between the two islands is spanned by centuries of tradition and kinship. Many are the seafaring stories that connect them. This is but one, and storytellers from the Glens of Antrim to the Isle of Skye have been putting their own twist on it for many years. There are a few variations in print (see Further Reading at the end of the book) but this is the bleakest I have come across. (R81.57. 26/2/81)

Many years ago, fishermen from Rathlin used to go over to Islay with boatloads of salted fish to sell and barter. The Islay men did likewise at different times and traded along the north-east coast of Ireland. Like all seafarers, the islanders always watched the weather and often complained about it. There was never just the right amount of wind to fill their sails. There was either not enough, which made for hard rowing or, worse still, there was too much, which brought about peril and distress.

Little wonder then that the fishermen kept an eye for even the slightest hint that would help them forecast wind and wave. Seagulls flying high above the island foretold a good breeze. When the oyster-catchers – those delightful black and white shore birds with bright red beaks – flew inland and picked through the farmers' fields, it warned of heavy rain and a coming gale. The arrival of woodcock and snow buntings in winter meant settled, freezing weather.

When house spiders worked like the Devil, hoarding wee flies and cocooning them in silk to hide up in the corner of the window sashes, you could stake your life that a really big storm that might last a week or a fortnight was on its way.

Cats were good weather forecasters too. An old cat suddenly sporting herself like a kitten was a sure sign of unsettled weather to come. One sitting with its back to the fire meant a storm was not far away. If the fire showed a flicker of blue then you could have no doubt the cat was right.

Even the weather could forecast the weather! If the fishermen saw a bonnet of mist down low on Knocklayde Mountain over on the mainland, they knew the weather was coming up from the south-west and would clear away to the north-east. In the summertime when the mist rose up like smoke over Murlough Bay, someone would always comment, 'I see Seamus O'Shiel is burning kelp the day', and the reply would come back, 'Aye, there'll be a bit of rain later this evening.'

Anyway, this one time there were a few boatloads of Rathlin folk over on Islay for a fair. They traded all their salted fish and stocked up on what provisions were offered: potatoes and barley oats and maybe a bottle or two of whiskey. They said their farewells and set out from Port Ìlein (Port Elleen) in a light breeze but even that soon fell away. With no wind at all they were going to have a long, back-breaking row home. They had no choice but to return to Islay.

'We didnae expect tae see ye back so soon,' said an Islay man on the quay.

'Aye, well, there's not a breath of wind out there the day,' replied a skipper of one of the Rathlin boats.

'Ye may go a see the woman who can rise the wind. Take a few coppers to pay her and she'll sort ye oot.'

It turned out that this woman was an old henwife who had a charm. She gave one of the Rathlin skippers a small leather bag with a piece of string dangling out.

'Now when ye want a wee breeze, pull on this string until you come to a knot. Untie the knot and you'll get your breeze. If ye want more wind, pull it again and untie another knot. Ye can't go wrong.'

So, off the Rathlin Islanders went back down to their boats and set sail again. The skipper with the charm was very wary at first but after the first knot he got a breeze and after one or two more they were sailing along quite nicely. 'By japers, this is working a treat,' he said to himself. The other boats were following along behind, and the women and children were sitting up in the bow sheltering from the spray under sheets of sail cloth. As they neared Rathlin they steered around into Church Bay and got home safe and sound.

A few months later they were all going to a fair on Islay again, and the skipper went to the woman for another charm. On the way back to Rathlin he used it as before. But whether he dropped the bag or discarded it, thinking he had no further use for it, no one knows, but didn't one of the children get their hands on it. It was a wee boy and he pulled out the string and with his wee teeth unfastened the knots one after the other. The wind rose steadily until it was blowing a living gale. The skipper could not fathom what was wrong, for the following boats seemed to be in a nice steady wind behind him. Not until it was too late did he realise what had happened. The boat capsized and the women and children and all were thrown into the sea.

One of the following boats picked up a couple of survivors but most were drowned. Never again did the seafaring men of Rathlin rely on otherworldly charms. They turned back to their old ways of forecasting the weather, taught to them by their fathers and grandfathers. And they trusted to their own seamanship.

THE PEAT CUTTER

For as long as anyone can remember there has been a dearth of good natural firing on Rathlin. It was always said that the Vikings cut all the trees to make repairs to their boats and the rest had long ago been burned. Peat was not as plentiful as it was in bogs on the mainland and not worth the effort of winning. Any driftwood that was washed in from time to time was quickly gathered by those who lived closest to the shore. Mostly the folk burned what they called cac bó – cow shit! The cow pats were left to harden off for a few days in the sun before being gathered and stacked to dry a little more. By all accounts it burned reasonably well with a very distinct smell not unlike that of damp wood smoke. This is another story of the underdog triumphing over his oppressive master. (R81.57. 26/2/81 & R81.63. 1/3/81)

As coal became available to the Rathlin Islanders, some people began to turn their noses up at those who still burned cac bó – the dried cow shit. It came to be thought of as old-fashioned and uncouth. People began to gather it at night and hide the stacks away behind outbuildings. They only burned it during the hours of darkness when the neighbours wouldn't see or smell the smoke. At last, only the very poorest or least-proud families gathered and burned it. It became a source of such shame that even the children who were sent out to collect it were mortified if anyone saw them.

One young girl who was returning along the road with a big two hundred weight-sized corn sack full of the stuff, which actually was very light in its sun-dried state, was stopped by a well-meaning and curious visitor to the island.

'What are you carrying in your sack miss?' she asked innocently.

Thinking on her feet and ashamed to reveal the real fruits of her morning's labour, the young girl replied, 'Limpets.'

'Limpets!' said the visitor looking at the size of the sack in amazement and imagining the weight of such a burden of heavy shellfish. 'My word, you young island girls must be very strong indeed.'

The very poorest of the poor, who could neither afford coal nor collect enough driftwood or cac bó, occasionally turned to cutting scraw – the top layer of peaty sod on the hill held together by heather roots. The cutting of scraw was forbidden by Gage the landlord. Some wryly observed this was because as the sole coal merchant on the island he was protecting his business. In truth, he could foresee, quite rightly, that once the scraw was removed it would allow wind and rain to wash away what little soil and grazing there was.

Through sheer want, one old man disobeyed his landlord. He cut away at the scraw. First it was just a few and then working around and around it was no time before he had a big brown circle cut into the top of the hill. Gage sent his land agent to inquire, though he knew fine well what was going on.

'You have been cutting scraw from the hill,' said the agent to the old man.

'Aye, for I've no firing you see or money to buy coal.'

'Well, Mr Gage says you'll have to put an end to it,' said the agent.

'But I have young grandchildren in the house and the nights are perishing.'

'Well, if you cut any more, Mr Gage will evict ye and put you off the island.'

The family were in a desperate plight, for they already owed rent and with nothing to burn in the fire and winter coming what were they to do? The old man went to the parish priest for advice, but he just told him to go along the shore and collect what driftwood he could find.

At that time there was a travelling missionary staying with the priest and when he heard about the plight of the old man and his family he went to see them.

'Take me up to this piece of ground till I see it,' he said to the old man.

'We better not father,' he said, 'for if the neighbours see us going up there they'll tell Gage's man.'

'Never mind about Gage or his man,' said the missionary. 'Take me up.'

Up they went and the missionary looked all around the hill where the old man had been cutting the scraw. He knelt down and whispered a few prayers and blessed the place. Then he asked to be taken back down. Before he bid the old man farewell, he spoke to him solemnly.

'As long as your family lives on this land, cut away at the scraw and trust that no harm will ever come to you.'

After the missionary priest left the island the old man was still very loathe to go against the landlord, but with no firing and cold as it was, his family were suffering. At last, he could stick it no longer and up he went and began to cut. It was hard work but eventually he filled a couple of creels and late that night he brought them down home and lit the fire. But someone was watching. A deceitful and heartless neighbour, who thought he might get the wee farm along with his own after the old man and his family were evicted, informed Gage's man.

The agent came barging in the following day. Smoke was drifting up the old man's chimney and the earthy smell of burning peat hung on the air. There was no way to hide the scraw.

'You were warned not to be cutting any more scraw,' said the agent.

'And neither I did,' answered the old man defiantly, for he had nothing to lose.

'Then where did you get these?' asked Gage's man.

'They were left over from before.'

'If I go up and see you have been cutting,' said the agent, 'I'll be back, and you'll be evicted this very day and put off the island.'

'Look away. I'm telling ye the truth,' he said, but to himself he thought, 'I'm done for.'

In an hour's time he saw the agent coming back down the hill and on towards the Manor House, but no word of eviction came.

Well, the neighbour swore blind that he had seen the old man come home with creels full of scraw, but there was no sign of any more workings. Again and again and again the old man went up and cut the scraw, and time after time the neighbour informed on him. But whenever Gage's man came to inspect the hill, he found nothing out of the ordinary – everything was always as before. Eventually, Mr Gage began to suspect that the tale-telling neighbour was only a damned nuisance out to cause trouble and so *he* was evicted and put off the island instead.

Just as the missionary had told him to do, the old man cut away at the scraw until his dying day. Never another word was said to him, though folk always wondered how he kept the fire burning and why the smell of peat smoke hung around his cabin.

THE COURIG GLASHIN

At one time, every man on Rathlin was a fisherman but not every man had a boat of his own. Some had shares in a boat. Some just lent a hand and got a share of the catch. And some men preferred to fish from the shore. The shore fishermen fished with lines and nets – draught nets mostly. These would be dragged up onto a beach and the men had to go out into the water up to their necks behind the net to make sure the fish did not escape. Everyone would then share the catch. This is a powerful tale, the wisdom of which resonates even today. (R81.57. 26/2/81)

Some Rathlin men shared a net among them up on the north-east end of the island. It was called the Courig Net after the place and the fish caught there were called Courig Glashin. They were the black pollock that were very common around that part of the coast.

The same net was shared by two neighbouring crews from the townland of Cleggan and a wee place called Brockley. One night the Cleggan boys would fish first and the Brockley boys second, and the next night Brockley would go first and Cleggan second. Whatever crew went first always got the biggest catch but working turn about as they did there was never any problem. It was the only fair way they could share out the fish and there was always plenty for everyone.

For donkey's years their system worked without any upset or argument, but then one time they were not able to fish for a few weeks because of rough weather. Somehow or another they got mixed up about whose turn it was and then they fell out over it. The Cleggan boys were sure it was their turn to go first but the Brockley boys said no it was theirs and neither would back down. They argued and fought. Neighbours stopped speaking to neighbours. The bitterness went deeper and deeper and soon no one was speaking to anyone.

How they settled the argument no one now remembers. But by the time they did it was too late. The net was fished a few times after that, but the Glashin were gone. As the old folk always used to say,

'If ye fall out over the fish, they'll leave and never come back.' And that's what happened. But for a wee bit of wit and generosity, Cleggan boys and Brockley boys might be fishing their net for the big Courig Glashin yet.

THE RATHLIN FAERIES

Just as in other parts of Ireland, it was well known on Rathlin that bad luck would follow anyone foolish enough to offend the faerie folk. For instance, most people had the good sense to leave faerie thorns well enough alone. The haw-thorn or whitethorn tree – which never grows to anything other than a large wind-sculpted shrub on Rathlin – is as common all over the island as it is on the mainland. It has long been planted to mark field boundaries and to keep stock in. Its old wood burns near as good as coal, but it never grows in such quantity as would produce enough for everyday firing.

The faerie thorn is the same type of tree, but one that grows naturally on its own – often in the middle of a field – unhindered by man. Beloved of the faerie folk, they were always left undisturbed to become ancient, gnarly specimens of their kind. Generations of folk have feared and revered these trees. Farmers have plough around them. Even to lift the fallen dead branches of a faerie thorn was unthinkable. To cut a live branch or, worse still, to fell a faerie thorn, would bring terrible misfortune. Here are combined three differing and, in the latter two, quite dark examples of faerie stories. (C79.29. 16/7/79 & R80.14. 15/2/80)

There was once a farmer, gull that he was, who took to cutting down a faerie thorn on his land to make the field bigger and give more graz-ing to his cattle.

'You better not cut that thorn,' said a neighbouring woman well known for being wise.

'Ah,' said the farmer, 'I don't care for all that old superstitious nonsense.'

'You'll care when the faeries knock the guts out of your cows.'

The farmer paid no heed and cut down the tree. At milking time that evening, his daughter came running into the yard.

'Da. Da. Come quick. There's something wrong with one of the cows.'

The beast was passing blood in her water – what the farmers called mewal. That night his best milker died. The next night there was another and so it went on.

'What am I going to do at all?' cried the farmer to his neighbour. 'I'll be ruined.'

'I warned ye,' she said, 'The only thing ye can do now is take two or three pounds in silver and leave it on the stump of the faerie thorn and maybe the wee folk will forgive ye.'

Two pounds of silver was a lot of money in them days but the farmer was desperate. He gathered up the silver and did as the old woman advised, and sure enough no more of his poor cows died. His livelihood was saved but he paid dearly for his foolishness.

Another young fellow, who cut down a faerie thorn just for the sheer devilment of it went, to gather seabirds' eggs on the cliffs at Kebble two or three days later. He fell to his death.

Faerie vengeance could be very spiteful and often severe. But the cruellest act of faerie revenge ever known on the island was visited on a poor hard-working family, and for a slight that many might have considered of no consequence – but the faeries thought otherwise.

It was a lovely Sunday evening in mid-summer, and a young girl was coming home from visiting relatives at the far end of Rathlin. Her dwelling was in the middle of the island, so she hadn't very far to go. She was taking her time enjoying the warm air when she heard music playing. It was very strange music, almost like harps and pipes and singing all together, but at the same time it was like nothing she had ever heard before. She followed the sound, dying to know where it was coming from or who could be playing such beautiful strains. She got to the top of a hill and looked down over into a wee hollow and there she saw where the music was coming from. It was faerie folk – laughing and dancing and enjoying themselves till their wee hearts were content.

The old folk of the island always used to say that if you heard faerie music you were never to look, for the wee folk got awful offended if they thought you were spying on them. But the young girl had no more sense, for she was only about 12 years old. She was drawn to the music like a moth to a flame and never thought she was doing a pin of harm. She watched the faerie folk dancing and carrying on for ages, and what a delightful and rare sight it was. Suddenly, one of them ran up the hill towards her. He stood in front of her for a few moments

with his wee red face like thunder. And then he turned and ran back down again, and the faeries disappeared.

Overjoyed by her chance encounter, the young girl ran all the way home. The first person she met was her grandmother, who she told breathlessly with excitement.

'Ah, no dear,' said the grandmother wringing her hands, 'You shouldn't have looked. This'll bring trouble to our door. Maybe they didn't see you. Did they see you?'

'Oh, they saw me alright Granny,' said the young girl.

'Och, are ye sure darlin'?'

'I'm sure Granny. One of them ran up the hill and stood there looking at me.'

'Did he say anything. What was he wearing?'

'He never said a word Granny – just stood there. I think he was wearing black.'

'Black! Oh, dear God of heaven, that means a death. Don't mention this to a soul now – do ye hear?'

'I won't Granny,' said the young girl, petrified now.

You see, the old folk said if you chanced to see the faeries it depended what colour they were wearing whether you got good luck or bad. White usually meant good but black was always bad.

A few days later, the whole family was away at the shore gathering seaweed to burn for kelp to pay their rent. The young girl was left at home to mind her wee brother, who was not yet 4. As well as that, she was given a list of chores to do before the family came back. She had to bake the bread, feed the hens, collect the eggs, milk the cow and tidy the place.

While the young girl worked away in the house, her little brother was quite content playing on the floor with a set of fire tongs. He was mesmerised by them the way children are with some things when they're wee. Ever since he was a baby they had always been set across his cradle to keep the faeries from stealing him – for the wee folk are heart feared of iron. Other families used their own means to keep their young children safe. A string with three knots to signify the Holy Trinity was a favourite on the island, and all mothers used deep cradles to make it harder for mischievous faeries to steal their babies.

With the milk cooling in the crock, the bread resting on the rack and the fire well tended, the young girl went out to feed the chickens in the yard and gather the eggs. 'Stay you here,' she told her wee brother, for she knew he would only get in the way. But when she came back to the house he was gone. She called his name and searched everywhere but not a trace of him could she find. By this time the family were beginning to arrive home, and she hoped to God he had wandered down to the road and been met by them, but no. No one had seen him. So, then everyone joined in the search.

They found the prints of his wee bare feet in mud near the byre and the mark of the fire tongs he was trailing along behind him. With their hearts in their mouths, they followed the tracks like hunters down a lane and around the side of a nearby lough. Eventually they led to a crag that tumbled away to the shore below. God love the wee child – it was there they found his little broken body.

His big sister lived to be a very old woman on the island, but she never got over that terrible ordeal. She always blamed herself, you see, for if she had not spied on the faeries that lovely summer Sunday evening, they would not have lured her innocent wee brother away to his death.

CEILIDHS AND CUSTOMS

As with all close-knit communities, people not born and bred into them are often at a disadvantage. No matter how long they might live among their adoptive community, they are always considered blow-ins. There used to be all kinds of little customs and quirks unique to the islanders that a blow-in might never fully get to grips with. And if the faerie folk were easily offended, Rathlin people could be as well, and their wrath, though maybe not as cruel, could be every bit as bewildering to the unwitting offender. The following are two examples of such tales that well might have their origins in truth. (R80.14 & 15. 15/2/80)

There was once a mainland woman living on Rathlin. She was the wife of a lightkeeper who came to work on the island. For many years they lived happily and became part of the Rathlin community. When the lightkeeper died, his wife stayed on.

One Saturday night, some of the neighbours came to ceilidh – to visit and tell stories and such. As the evening wore on the craic was mighty and the lightkeeper's widow decided it was time to make a drop of tae and a wee bite of supper for her guests. She got up and set the big black kettle on the hob of the fire. The spout happened to be pointing in the direction of a particular wee woman, who bounced up out of her chair like a hen off her nest and flew out the door, near taking it off the hinges as she left. None of the neighbours passed any remark and, although the lightkeeper's widow felt there was a wee bit of an atmosphere, she just thought her friend had been taken short or was feeling suddenly unwell.

The next morning, the widow woman was going down the road to her place of worship when she saw her neighbouring friend. She hailed her but the woman acted as if she was blind and never looked towards the road the widow was on. Mystified, she mentioned it to another woman who was in the company that evening.

'Did I say something out of turn the other night – something to offend?' she asked.

'Oh no dear,' said the other woman. 'It's just you pointed the spout of the kettle at her.'

Not understanding the gravity of her offence, it had to be explained to the widow that it was always the way on Rathlin that visitors were never asked to leave. If members of the household wanted to discuss some family business among themselves or with a particular neighbour, they would point the spout of the kettle at whoever they wanted to depart. Without a word, the individual would take the hint and his or her leave.

And that was how the lightkeeper's widow innocently offended her neighbour. It could have been worse, for if she had wound up the mantle clock she could have inadvertently offended everyone. That was the unspoken sign for the whole company to leave!

Years before this wee incident, another lightkeeper living on the island found a seal washed up on the shore. He went for his knife to butcher the animal, for the blubber – once rendered down into oil – was used for everything from rubbing into aching joints to burning in cruise lamps. From the pelt he intended to make tobacco pouches or some waterproof garment. Just as the lightkeeper was about to start his gory business, an old beachcombing islander happened upon him.

'What the hell are you playing at boy? Are ye mad?' shouted the islander.

'What? I'm just making good use of this seal,' said the keeper. 'What harm's in it?' he added defensively, for he thought the island man was about to fight.

'I tell ye what harm's in it. That seal could be one of us.'

Well, the lightkeeper thought the old man was mad or drunk, until he was told the story.

'Years ago, this island man was out hunting seals. He saw a cow on the beach and knew there must be a newborn nearby. Their wee pure white pelts used to fetch good money. As the man went forward to kill the little one, the cow raised its fin and shouted, "Donal, Donal, don't kill my child."

'The man's heart nearly stopped, for then and there he knew the seal had been here before and was one of us. Ever since that day, no man on Rathlin has ever harmed a seal. Any that get washed up on the shore are buried with the same respect we would bury one of our own – for who knows, they just might be kin!'

ELIZA BROWN AND THE HIRELING

Another custom faithfully observed by Rathlin Islanders concerned the bury-
ing of human remains washed up around their coast. For such a small mass of
land, many ill-fated seafarers were washed ashore. Most were interred just as
they were found – clothes and all. Should they have had a thousand pounds in
their possession or been dripping with jewels, they went into the ground just as
they were. It was thought to be unlucky to take anything from a body brought
in by the tide, and seven een by some as a great wickedness that would bring
misfortune to the whole island. (R80.15. 15/2/80)

In 1870, a ship called the *Cambria* sailing from New York to Glasgow
struck Tor Beg rock, half a mile north-west of Inishtrahull Island, which
is about 6 miles north-east of Malin Head. Aboard were 179 souls. Only
one man survived. A few days later, the body of a wealthy woman
washed ashore at the far end of Rathlin. Her name was Eliza Brown and
she was wearing gold rings and jewels, and a money belt full of dollars.

A young fellow hired in from the mainland by a Rathlin farmer as
a herds boy found her. He stole the money belt and tried to slip the
woman's rings off, but her corpse was too badly swollen. So, the brute
used a sharp rock to smash and sever her fingers and take the rings.
He might have been lynched if he had not escaped from the island
before his terrible crime was discovered. Within a week he was on a
ship bound for America, no doubt to get as far away from Rathlin as
he could, his passage paid for by his ill-gotten gains.

Some months later, a rich relative of Eliza Brown came to Rathlin.
As the people told him the story of what had taken place, they took
great pains to make clear that the culprit was not one of theirs but a
hireling from the mainland. Even so, they felt a great weight of shame
because of what had happened to her on their island. Before the man
left he erected a large gravestone to Ms Brown's memory.

THE OUTCAST RETURNED

Gage the landlord appears in many of TC's island stories as a very strict and intolerant master. This short tale reveals, yet again, the islanders' delight in and need for situations where one of their own gets the better of their oppressive overlord – a common motif in folk tales throughout Ireland and other places. This story may even have its origins in historical fact – will we never know. (R80.15. 15/2/80)

There was once a young fellow who was up to all sorts of mischief and mayhem on the island. Complaints were made about this holy terror of a lad who was stealing and destroying all around him. Eventually Gage could take no more, and he banished the miscreant from the island. As he was being manhandled aboard a boat that would take him to the mainland, he defiantly spat abuse and obscenities at Gage.

'You're getting rid of me today you old rogue, but I'll be back, dead or alive, within a month. You mark my words. I'll be back.'

And so, he ranted and raved like a madman from the departing boat until his voice was little more than a faint cry on the wind.

Anyway, the young fellow got to the mainland, and he took a notion he would go to America to seek his fortune. He got on a ship in Belfast bound for New York and the first day out they were hit by an easterly gale. The ship was wrecked on the lower east coast of Rathlin and, as always, Gage went down to the shore to make sure the islanders did not purloin anything that was his. Being landlord and owner, he enjoyed all the rights of salvage.

In the midst of the crashing waves and swirling winds, who should come ashore like a bilge rat and him more dead than alive, but the young fellow Gage had banished just a week or two before.

'Didn't I tell ye I would return within a month,' he roared at his landlord through the gale, his eyes dancing with blatant devilish delight.

The young fellow lived to be a very old man and in all his life he never left Rathlin again. He was always a thorn in Gage's side, but why the landlord suffered him to stay on the island no one could understand. Being a truly God-fearing man first and foremost, Gage maybe thought that the young fellow's miraculous homecoming was nothing short of divine providence and not something that even he should dare to rule against.

AN CAPALL CAILÍN

In days gone by, many of the island loughs, it was said, were home to a capall uisce – a water horse. An Capall Ban – the White Horse – comes to mind (Stories and Legends of Rathlin, Augustine McCurdy, 2006). Known as kelpies in Scotland, these spirit creatures were wont to prey on unwary humans, especially young women, at night and take them back down into the cold, dark depths of their lough for purposes unspecified! TC referred to this creature as Capercallion, which I took to come from Capall Cailín – Horse of the Colleen. In other versions of this tale by Rathlin tellers, the term Creannan Dubh is used to describe a black stallion with a white nose flash. (R80.15. 15/2/80)

At one time, the Rathlin landlord outcast any young girl who was unfortunate enough to become pregnant out of wedlock. No appeals were entertained, though many were offered, but none were so strange and terrifying as those from girls who claimed to have been the victim of an Capall Cailín – the Horse of the Colleen.

Just like the other spirit horses, this was a wild and fearsome stallion, but it also had a great horn that grew out from its breast. Some islanders used to say, perhaps with roguish humour, that this beast was very particular in its taste for it especially desired the young unmarried womenfolk of one family. I daren't mention the name, for this part of the story might not be true and would only cause offence to descendants living on the island yet. In any case, once assailed by the Capall Cailín, these poor young innocent women were always left with child and, of course, that meant banishment from the island.

The family seemed cursed, but then one night a young woman of the clan took matters into her own hands. Instead of running away from the feared beast when it stalked her, she stood her ground. As the Capall Cailín charged her at full gallop, she goaded it on. At the last moment, she bounded up on to a stone wall. In its wild fury the beast's horn stuck the stones and drove it back into its own heart, killing it instantly.

The next day, they buried the Capall Cailín under a cairn of stones and never again did it bedevil that clan or indeed any other young women of the island. Whether those unmarried womenfolk became less disposed to getting themselves in the family way after these events, I wouldn't like to say.

A SECRET OF THE CHILDREN OF LIR

In Irish legend 'The Fate of the Children of Lir' is one of 'The Three Sorrows of Storytelling' – 'Truagha na Scealaidheachta'. It has been told the length and breadth of the country for generations and was a favourite on Rathlin too. Less often told are stories of some of the many adventures and people the Children of Lir met with during their three hundred years of exile on the Sea of Moyle. This is but one. (R80.17. 17/2/80)

A poor Rathlin fisherman out trying to get a few fish to feed his family heard beautifully sorrowful singing coming across the uneven waves. He was drawn by the sound away out into the Sea of Moyle, further than he ever went before. Eventually, he came upon four pure white swans drifting together and found the source of the music. It was Fionnuala singing to her young siblings – Aodh, Fiachra and Conn.

Although the poor fisherman was hungry, and swans were considered a great delicacy by some, he spared the beautiful creatures for he knew they must be enchanted. The fisherman spoke to the swans kindly and Fionnuala answered.

'We dare not venture near land for fear we will be killed and eaten,' she said.

'I can help you,' said the fisherman. 'Come with me and I will show you a cave where you can shelter from all but an easterly wind.'

Fionnuala was wary at first, but the old man was so gentle, and she and her siblings had suffered so much already, she decided to trust him. The cave was on the north-east corner of Rathlin and was as the old fisherman had described.

'It will do for tonight for we are weary,' said Fionnuala, 'but we cannot stay longer. If a swell should come from the east we would be swept up into the cave and dashed against the rocks or drowned.'

'Fear not,' said the fisherman, 'I know someone who will help.'

The fisherman returned the next morning with a woman to whom he had told the story. She was said to possess charms and powers of transformation but, like all her kind, she seemed unable to improve her own fortune.

The woman was able to work a spell that raised a great ledge of rock from the depths and set it across the entrance of the cave. This barrier kept waves from crashing into the opening and the waters within lay quiet and calm. It was here that the Children of Lir often came at high tide to seek sanctuary from the worst storms of winter.

With her good deed done, the woman hurried home to her young son, who had never seen the light of day. He had been blinded as a small child and never strayed far from their cabin. As the woman wearily traipsed up the hill she suddenly lifted her head. There, standing in the road was her son, gazing at the sky and every passing cloud and bird and bee with great delight, for his eyesight had somehow been restored.

For his kindness and good grace, the fisherman too was well rewarded. From that day on, never did he have to travel far to fill his

net with fish. He and his family enjoyed a life of plenty and always he gave thanks to the Children of Lir for his blessings. Wasn't it well for the poor fisherman that Fionnuala had been brought up to believe that every good turn is deserving of another?

It was because of this story and others like it that swans came to be revered on Rathlin. Even when the people were afflicted by great hunger and hardship, still they could not bring themselves to harm these most enchanting of birds.

RAVENS AND RIVALRY

In these little sketches the raven, as usual, appears as a villain. On Rathlin, as in other parts of the country, ravens and their cousins, the hooded crows and magpies, have always been persecuted mercilessly. Sadly, jackdaws, rooks and the charming little chough, a red-beaked, red-legged, and much rarer member of the corvid family once found on Rathlin, have all suffered by being mistaken for their carrion-eating cousins. Birds of a feather do not always flock together! (C79.32 18/7/79)

Ravens have long been despised on Rathlin Island. One old island slant on a famous Bible story might go a little way to explain the contempt with which these birds were once held. According to the Book of Genesis, it was after forty days and forty nights that Noah sent out a raven. The bird flew here and there but did not return. Only then did Noah release a dove, which eventually returned with a sprig of olive leaves.

In those far-off days, the raven's plumage was as white and unblemished as that of the swan. But when it flew away from the ark and found the corpses of all the dead people and animals drowned by the rising waters, it was overcome by temptation and gorged itself on rotting flesh. Seeing this and the raven's pure white plumage marred by blood and gore, Noah cursed the bird, saying it would never know any peace. Ever since then, its feathers have been tainted by the colour of death and ravens have been the most unloved of birds.

Since time out of memory, the folk of the lower, south-east end of the island have referred to those from the upper, west end as 'Birds'. This probably relates to the great seabird colonies at Kebble and insinuates the Birds' tendency to be wild, noisy and foul smelling. Likewise, the Birds referred to those from the lower end as 'Cuddens' after a little fish that shoals in and around the harbour at Church Bay. The Cuddens are caught easily and not much good for anything! Nowadays this little display of tribalism is, at worst, a tongue-in-cheek rivalry, but in days gone by folk were easily offended by such name-calling. Could this have been the cause of a fight that once took place between two Rathlin chieftains? Or was the fight the start of the rivalry between the Birds and the Cuddens?

In any case, the story goes that two warriors clashed with sword and shield and half killed each other. One was a chief from the upper end of the island, the other from the lower end. The chief from the upper end had his belly cut open and his innards began to spill out. As he tried to hold himself together and make his way home, a villainous raven attacked him. To get away from it he crawled to some caves, but the damage was done. The place where the warrior perished was named after him as O'Byrne. It is said that in his mortal agony, his fingers gouged out marks in the limestone wall, the trace of which can still be seen to this day.

THE FIRST RAVENS

For a thousand years the folk of Rathlin have lost no love for the raven – the bird that once stood as a symbol for their most hated of enemies. But in Norse mythology ravens were revered above all other birds and long associated with Odin – God of wisdom, healing, death, battle and many other things. Vikings were said to carry ravens with them on their long voyages. When no land could be seen on the horizon, they would release a bird or two and then follow on. The ravens always guided them to the nearest dry land. Perhaps this scrap of lore points to the origin of the following story. (C79.32. 18/7/79)

It's many years ago that the crew of a Viking longship intending to land on Rathlin and plunder whatever they could got caught in a fierce swirling tidal race. The islanders gathered to watch as the Norsemen struggled to free themselves. It quickly dawned on them what the islanders already knew – their longship was doomed. Even if the Norsemen abandoned their vessel and somehow survived the raging waters, they would be slaughtered as they came ashore exhausted and unarmed.

While the islanders looked on, the Viking captain suddenly ran to the prow of his ship. With his sword he began to cut free the intricately carved figurehead. It was in the shape of a huge black bird with a knowing eye and fearsome heavy beak. Then he ordered his men to pile everything that would burn in the middle of their vessel – pitch, wooden oars, ropes and sails. He set light to it and made a great crackling bonfire of it all.

As the flames leapt higher into the threatening grey skies, one by one the warriors stepped forward, raised their swords in the air and threw themselves onto their funeral pyre. Their cries of agony could be heard all over Rathlin. The stench of their burning flesh was carried on the wind, and yet not one their number flinched. At last, their captain heaved the ship's figurehead onto the fire and, calling out a prayer to Odin, the Raven God of the Norsemen, he too pitched

himself upon the flames with one last defiant cry. As he did so, a thick cloud of dark smoke swirled around the fire and the figurehead slowly transformed into a great black-winged beast. As it rose up, the islanders cowered in fear.

Then the spirit of each Viking warrior arose from the smoke and took the shape of a shining black raven. The birds uttered harsh, echoing croaks and caws, the like of which no one had heard before. They flew straight to the island and the people were in great dread of them.

Ever after, these birds fed on the corpses of dead animals. They stole the seabirds' eggs from the cliffs and robbed lambs from ewes as they gave birth. They gathered on battlefields and at funerals – always attendants where death stalked.

Once unknown on Rathlin, ravens prospered, and to this day they are to be found in every corner of the island. These were the first of their kind on Irish soil and they are still plundering and casting bad blood and fear as their Viking ancestors used to do all those years before.

THE SEALS OF DÚN NA GAEL

Up near the most northerly point, on the west side of the island, is an ancient, fortified outcrop of rock known as Dún Mór – Big Fort – which has long since tumbled down. Below is a narrow rocky inlet where the first Vikings were said to have landed on Rathlin, and Ireland! This place was once known as Dún na Gael – Fort of the Gael. Seals were always seen around the mouth of the inlet, swimming and lying on a large rock there. The story of why this should be so was a favourite with the old storytellers of Rathlin. (C79.32. 18/7/79)

A chieftain once lived in Dún Mór on Rathlin. He had a son, and long had the young man dreamed of sailing to the enchanted isle that lay far to the west. The isle only appeared every seven years and it was said by the old folk that the king of this isle had once visited Rathlin many years before. They said he had a beautiful daughter and that he had made a pledge that if any mortal man could land on his isle he would grant him his daughter's hand.

This promise was almost too good to be true, but the chieftain's son thought on it day and night until at last he set sail for the enchanted isle with a crew of Rathlin men. After many days and nights of sailing eventually they came upon it. It was swathed in thick clouds of sea mist. Treacherous reefs and swirling currents surrounded the barren shores that faded in and out of view. It was impossible to land without being wrecked.

The only signs of life around the isle were the seals that swam in the dark waters. They were said to be enchanted and could speak in human tongues. In desperation, the young man hailed one of them to his boat.

'Can you help us find a way onto the land?' he asked.

'I can help. but you must help us in return,' said the seal.

The creature showed the young man the only way to get on and off the isle.

'Is not the king of this isle welcoming?' asked the young prince.

'He is a treacherous man. We seals are the enchanted souls of men taken by the sea, but we are captives here. Our kin are killed and eaten by the people of this isle. Be warned, they will not take kindly to you.'

And neither they did, for no one had ever come to their island before and returned to tell the tale. The king ranted and raved like a madman.

'Leave my isle instantly or I will have you bound in irons and caged like an animal.'

'But I am here to claim your daughter as you promised,' said the young man.

Well, the king didn't get angry until then. His face turned white with rage, and he banished his daughter away to be incarcerated for showing her consent. He sent the young man away – only sparing him for fear his men might know the way on to his isle and come back to avenge their captain.

The young man returned to Rathlin empty-handed and disheartened. Night after night he went down from Dún Mór to the rocks at Dún na Gael. There he sat staring out to sea, lamenting the fact that the king of the enchanted isle had broken his promise.

One night the seal came to him. The young man recognised and greeted the creature.

'I have come to tell you how to gain your heart's desire.'

'I beg ye tell me now.'

'Land where I showed you. Bring with you a handful of soil from Rathlin and in your palm will be held great power, for if that soil should touch the isle, the enchantment will be broken. It would become as real and solid as your own island home. Use this against the king and he will release his daughter, but you must demand that my kin are released also. Do this and we will be forever in your debt.'

The chieftain's son did as the seal advised. After many trials and tribulations, he won the hand and heart of the old king's daughter and the sealfolk were released from their bondage.

The enchanted isle sank back into the sea not to be seen again for many years. The chieftain's son returned to Rathlin with his bride and the handful of Rathlin soil for, of course, he never used it – except to bargain for his bride. Whether the young couple lived happily for the rest of their days, no one now remembers. But the seals that came with them from the enchanted isle have lived around the little inlet below Dún Mór ever since. And they are there yet, faithfully guarding the entrance to Dún na Gael for the rest of time.

THE VANISHING ISLE

All along the north and west coast of Ireland (and Scotland) there are stories of an enchanted isle that only appears now and then, commonly every seven years, and then sinks back into the sea again. The land had various names including Hy-Brasail and Tír na nÓg – the Land of the Forever Young. Whatever the name, these magical islands were always described as a paradise where people never grew old and had everything they would ever need or want. There were various ways someone could gain access to or prevent the isle from disappearing. Throwing soil or live embers on to its shore were sure ways to achieve this. Rathlin has a very strong tradition of these stories. The following are two are unusual variants.

Many young Rathlin men dreamed of making their fortune by setting foot on the enchanted isle and claiming it for themselves. One or two came very close. On a calm summer's day, a young fellow rowed out from Rathlin and eventually came to a beautiful isle on which grew strange palms and fruit trees, the like of which he had only heard old mariners speak. The groves were neat and well tended, and everything looked green and plentiful. In among the tall shrubbery, the young fellow caught glimpses of magnificent houses built of shining white marble and palaces with golden domes and spires. He could hear music playing and laughter and was sure he had found the enchanted isle.

On and on he rowed, and the currents seemed to pull him ever closer, but he could find nowhere safe to land. 'If I could just get a foot on to those rocks,' he thought to himself. He came as close as he dared, for although it was calm the swell breaking against the sharp rocks would have wrecked his little currach. Eventually he saw a place where he thought he might just be able to jump ashore.

Thinking he would gain a better grip with his bare feet, the young fellow untied his muddy brogues and left them in the bottom of the boat. With his heart in his mouth, he leapt from the currach on to the rocks. Eyes closed and teeth gritted, he anticipated the sharp pain of his landing. What he felt was the shock of the freezing cold Atlantic

Ocean, for the moment his foot touched the rock, the island disappeared, and he was left floundering around in the open sea gasping for breath. Lucky for him, he could swim after a fashion and managed to get back into his boat. It was a long, cold row back home and as he told his strange story later that evening around the fire, his grandmother scolded him.

'Sure, what did ye take your brogues off for?' she said, 'The slightest bit of Rathlin clay would have been enough to break the enchantment and the island would have been yours for the taking!'

Another time, a young fellow came upon the island and rowed all around it. Like those who had come before, he could find nowhere to land. There were sheer cliffs running straight down into the sea, but through them ran seams of the purest gold. The young fellow could touch the precious yellow metal and it came away in his hands in great lumps. He filled a wicker creel with the nuggets, and with his boat ladened almost to the gunwales, he rowed for home.

Eventually he made it back to Rathlin and landed at a place on the north end called Altahora. He struggled to carry the creel up the steep cliff path so heavy it was, and he had to rest often. Late as he was, his father came looking for him and when he saw his son labouring up the path he called to him.

'What have ye in the creel son?'

'It's gold Da. I brought it from the enchanted isle.'

'Whatever ye do son, don't let it touch the ground,' his father cried anxiously.

On up the young fellow came, panting like a dog and the sweat breaking on him like a galloping horse. When he reached the top his limbs were trembling under the strain and his foot slipped on a rounded stone. He stumbled and let go the heavy creel. All the gold spilled out and as it rolled down the path it turned into a thousand seeds that drifted down to the shore on the breeze. Before the father and son's unbelieving eyes a fortune vanished, as did the enchanted isle and was not seen for many years again.

Where the seeds fell a strange palm-like plant grew. It flourishes there yet and is found nowhere else on the island. Even today, the people come to gather it for Palm Sunday.

THE THIRD WAVE

Coastal fishermen and seafarers all know that after a predictable number of waves one will be stronger than the rest. In many places it is seven strong waves, with the seventh being the biggest and most powerful. This is followed by calmer waves before the cycle repeats itself. On Rathlin they say that the waves always come in threes (see foreword by Linda-May Ballard). Around the island there are many dangerous reefs the islanders call 'bows' and huge seas coming in threes break over them with awe-inspiring relentlessness. This story has variants on the west coast of Ireland where the 'offender' may be taken beneath the waves to rectify his misdeed. (C79.32.18/7/79)

One day there were three fishermen – a father, his son and a neighbour – out in a small boat fishing close to the east shore of the island. As they were going around the coast they came to a bow with the waves crashing over it. Instead of going out around it, they decided that they could cut in between the reef and the mainland when the seas were calmer and save themselves some hard rowing. When they were halfway through, they saw a huge sea coming in and realised they had misjudged the waves.

'We're done for,' said the son.

'Pull away,' ordered the father from the stern. 'We'll be alright.'

'No point in rowing now,' cried the neighbour, 'we'll never clear that wave.'

'Pull away I tell ye,' shouted the father once more. 'We'll be alright if ye do as I say.'

As the mighty wave was bearing down on them and threatening to overwhelm their little boat, the father took a knife and hurled it behind him into the wave. The water seemed to part, and the wave passed harmlessly either side of them. As it did, so a woman rose up from the wave beside the boat. The blade of the father's knife was lodged in her breast.

'Draw your knife from me,' she called to the father.

'I will not,' he replied defiantly.

'Draw your knife or pay the price.'

The father steadfastly refused to draw the knife from the woman, for he knew that if he did they would all be lost. The price paid was that he never went to sea again. If he had ever dared to set foot in a boat again the woman of the wave would have claimed him and any who sailed with him.

The old ways of the sea are sometimes cruel and always mysterious to landsmen.

THE BRAVE BROTHER

There are other Rathlin stories where a warrior chief, either Viking or from some other island, comes into conflict with an islander of lower rank over the hand of a woman. Others end in much more tragic circumstances, but this story has a positive, if not entirely happy, final twist to it. (C79.32.18/7/79)

There was once a chieftain's daughter on Rathlin who was betrothed to marry a young chief from Islay. The princess did not want to marry him for she loved an island lad, but he was a poor fisherman and not good enough for the likes of her. Nevertheless, she declared her love for the fisherman and in so doing angered her father and slighted the chief from Islay. He vowed to come over to Rathlin and fight this young upstart in a duel to the death.

Over the Sea of Moyle the warrior came in a fury. The young fisherman was afraid, for he had never held a sword or a shield in his life. The Rathlin chieftain offered three blades for the opponents to choose from. Two of the swords were enchanted for, being old Viking weapons, they were useless in the hands of anyone other than a Norseman and would never draw blood again. Only one of the swords could strike a mortal blow. Being of higher birth, the Islay man was given the first choice and wasn't he fortunate enough to pick the uncorrupted blade. Truth was, he had been helped by an old hag on the island who told him which blades to refuse.

And so, the duel was set but the poor Rathlin fisherman did not stand a chance. On the morning of the fight, two combatants stepped out to face one another but instead of the poor fisherman his younger brother came to take his place.

'It matters not to me whether I fight a shameless coward or his fool of a stand in,' said the Islay chief. 'Blood will be drawn this day and satisfaction mine.'

The two men attacked each other like rutting stags. Though the bold Rathlin youth gave a good account of himself neither he nor his sword proved to be a match for the warrior from Islay. Within a short time, the young fellow fell to the ground mortally wounded. As he lay there, his lifeblood ebbing away, the Islay man finished him off with a dreadful cry of triumph.

That day the Rathlin princess and the Islay man were wed. The feasting and revelry lasted long into the night. The next morning, still reeling drunk from the wedding festivities, the Islay man took his young bride and with his men set off back across the Sea of Moyle to his own island home. As they rounded Bull Point at the western end of Rathlin a sudden violent wave overturned their boat. Drunk as he was, the Islay man perished within sight of the shore, but the Rathlin princess clung to the underside of the stricken vessel and called for help.

A fisherman tending his nets near the shore rowed to where the young woman was in peril and saved her life. And wasn't her saviour the poor fisherman whom she loved and had wanted to be with all along.

And didn't the pair become man and wife and by all accounts live very happily ever after. The old folk said it was foretold. But the fisherman often looked up to the stars at night and whispered a prayer of thanks for his brave young brother.

HEADLAND OF THE FAIR COLLEEN

Fair Head, with its Iron Age crannog towers 660ft above sea level, is the closest headland to Rathlin. The story of how it got its name has several variants. Here there are definite parallels with the story of the Rathlin princess, Taise, after which Glentaise is named, but which ends quite differently. The heroine of this story, however, is sometimes referred to as Taise and includes the anti-hero Nabgodon, the famous Norse king, though more commonly neither are named. It is a heart-rending tale in a sorrowful style comparable to, for example, 'Deirdre of the Sorrows'. (C79.32 18/7/79)

A thousand years ago and more, when the Kingdom of Dál Riada was at its height, there was a chieftain who ruled over Rathlin Island. He had a daughter who was famed for her beautiful flaxen hair and pale skin. She had been betrothed years before to the son of a faithful warrior of high rank, and though the two young lovers were very attached to one another, they were yet unwed.

But Vikings from the north came lusting after plunder and women-folk. The Rathlin chieftain tried to appease the intruders by offering hospitality and treating them like welcome visitors. This worked for a while, but their hunger and thirst could not be sated. They wanted more than their innards greased with salmon and seabirds and their gizzards wet with wine.

One day, the leader of the Viking marauders beheld the chieftain's beautiful daughter with the flaxen hair and pale skin. He soon coveted her for his bride, but of course she was already betrothed. He could have ordered his men to fight for her, but there would have been much bloodshed for his hosts were not afraid to raise their swords and battle axes to defend their chieftain's honour.

The Viking knew the old chieftain did not want to fight, so he appealed to his wish for peace and offered a pact of friendship in return for his daughter's hand.

'Better that we two make an alliance by marriage than fight over a woman and weaken each other,' said the Viking.

It was a clever ploy for the Norseman to get what he wanted, as well as a dowry that could be shared with his warriors to satisfy their craving for plunder. The old chieftain peered into his adversary's cold blue eyes. He knew if he refused the proposal he would plunge his clan into a deadly conflict, and his young daughter might be taken by force anyway.

'I will consider your offer,' he said, 'but as you may know, she is already spoken for.'

When the chieftain told his daughter that he intended to give her away in marriage to the Viking she was distraught, of course. She wept and beat her fists on the walls, but she was no spoiled or whimpering child. Even in her anguish she understood the terrible consequences of her refusing a union with the Norseman.

'In your hands lie the lives of our warriors, their women and their children,' said the chieftain to his daughter with a sigh.

'I bow to your wishes and your wisdom father,' she said. 'But a great fear is on me. All will not end well.'

With that she hurried away back to her chamber to brood over her future.

When all was prepared for the wedding, a great fire was set alight on the clifftop at Dún Mór, and kinsmen came from all around. For days they feasted on salmon and shellfish and seabirds' eggs. Cattle and sheep were slaughtered, and the guests downed great skins of ale and mead and wine. When they were drunk, they kept on drinking until they were sober and then fell down drunk again.

But the Viking chief kept his wits about him and a tight eye on his new bride. It wasn't long before he noticed that she rarely looked in his direction. Instead, she seemed only to have eyes for one young warrior who sat behind his chieftain. He was handsome and there was a sadness in his eyes. His hand never strayed from the hilt of his sword, and he did not partake in any of the wantonness.

When the young bride slipped away from her husband's side and the young warrior moved back into the shadows, the Viking knew his wife was in danger of being unfaithful even before they had consummated their marriage. When he found the two lovers in an embrace, he drew his sword and cried out for vengeance. There was a mighty sigh of iron blades slipping from leather sheaths as Viking and Rathlin clansmen alike rose to fight. But the Viking chief bid them to put away their swords and be seated.

'This fight is between me and my wife's young tempter,' he said, 'I will have his blood, or he will have mine.'

And so, the two warriors clashed in mortal combat to the ring of iron and grunts of effort. The duel became a great spectacle to entertain the drunken horde. By the light of leaping flames and torches the cheering onlookers were mesmerised and they eventually fell silent.

The combatants were evenly matched for a while at least, but soon the older warrior began to tire, and the young Rathlin man gained the upper hand. He was first to draw blood – a deep gash across the Viking's breast. As the Norseman fell to the ground, he cried out in agony.

'Spare me! Spare me!'

The young warrior looked around the assembled warriors before grudgingly giving his adversary the mercy he seemed to be begging for. One liege ran to his fallen master's side. No one noticed the whispered exchange between dying Viking warlord and his loyal servant.

The father of the bride nodded for the musicians to play some lively music and more strong drink was quickly brought out for his guests. The tension so quickly raised by the skirmish seemed to wane in an instant as the music soared and the revellers turned back to their wild orgy of drinking and cavorting.

Before his flaxen-haired daughter could make her way through the throng to be by her lover's side, she was whisked off her feet and birled around and around. It was the Viking's faithful servant who held her in his arms as he flung her about as easily as if she were his own cloak. She cried out for him to release her, but those nearest howled with delight and urged them on to faster and faster spinning and turning.

As her father and brave young lover became alert to the distress she was in, it was too late. She was danced to the rocky precipice, where she and her whirling assassin pitched over and fell through the darkness to meet their deaths in the waves below Dún Mór. The last words she uttered to her father came back to haunt him, 'All will not end well.'

A day or two later, her broken body was found washed ashore on the mainland at the foot of the An Bhinn Mhór – the Great Cliff. In memory of the beautiful chieftain's daughter with the flaxen hair and pale skin, the place became known as Ceann Tíre an Cailín Fionn – Headland of the Fair Colleen. Over time the name was rendered into English and shortened to Fair Head.

Few who stand atop this grand outcrop of basalt on the north coast of Ireland give any thought to the ancient sad story that led to its naming. Instead, they watch with delight over the swirling sea and marvel at the stunning beauty of Rathlin Island beyond.

THE POT OF GOLD

In many Irish folk tales Vikings are characterised as barbarians capable only of violence and bloodshed, who almost always get their comeuppance. One element of this story, however, allows for a slightly different view. It is a recurring feature of similar stories that the Norsemen always repaid a good turn. But the main theme of this story, and others like it, is the folly and danger of wastefulness. The message still resonates with modern listeners and, I think, makes a great metaphor for the care and management of natural resources. (R80.29. 19/4/80)

A thousand years ago, Viking raiders came to Rathlin. There were skirmishes all over the island as the people tried to defend their farms and families. When the fighting was over many lay dead or dying.

One woman, who was already a widow, had lost the youngest of her three sons. As she searched through the heather to find his body she found the corpses of other young men. Even though many were her enemies, she was moved to bury them rather than let the ravens pick their bones clean.

'They are all someone's sons,' she said.

But then the woman came across a young man who was wounded. He was a Viking and about the same age as her own dead son. 'Now that my youngest son is gone,' she thought to herself, 'if I can nurture the Viking back to health he might prove himself of use with the fishing and the farming.' There and then she decided to steal the foreign warrior back to her own cabin and tend to his wounds.

To conceal him from her neighbours she dyed his light hair black with boiled lichen, and passed him off as her own. While he slowly gained his strength she taught him their native language. As they spoke, he told the woman that he was the son of a Viking king from Lochlainn.

'One day my father will be very grateful that you have saved my life,' he said.

After many months he was fit and able to start work. As the woman had hoped, he was as good as her own surviving sons, and they all worked happily together at the fishing and farming.

Time passed and one day the boys were out fishing together on the northside of the island. Suddenly they saw a big red sail approaching. The Viking ships were returning. The two Rathlin boys tried to row for the shore, but the longboat overhauled them. They would have all been killed, but the young Viking spoke to his country men in their own tongue.

'Spare them,' he said, 'These men are my brothers. Their mother saved my life.'

Well, the Vikings let the two islanders go home but they took their comrade with them and returned him to his father. When the two brothers told their mother what had happened, she thought for a long while.

'We will tell everyone your brother fell from the boat and was drowned,' she eventually said, and her sons obeyed.

A year and a day passed, and the Vikings returned once more. This time the Viking king came ashore and searched the island for the woman.

'Are you she who saved my son?' he asked.

'I am,' said she.

'Then I must reward your kindness. Ask anything and if it is within my power you will have it.'

'I don't want to be rich,' said the woman. 'I just want what will do me.'

'What will do you? But how much is that?' said the Viking.

'Well, enough to do me and my family our day,' said the woman.

The Viking went back to his ship to consult his wisemen. He returned the next day with a small clay pot.

'Take this.' he said, 'It will last you and your family all your days. But be warned, never take more from the pot than you need.'

With that, the Viking took his leave of Rathlin and the woman was left with the little clay pot. When she peered into it she could see a few small gold coins. Although she had never possessed anything like it in her whole life, it didn't look like it would last very long, never mind a lifetime. Be that as it may, the woman took the pot outside, buried it in the ground and covered it with a stone. Every now and then, whenever she wanted to buy a cow or a few more sheep, she would go to the pot and take a coin from it. In this way time passed, but the pot never seemed to empty.

As the years went by, the woman lived in comfort. Her sons married and built homes close by, and they too lived in comfort. But then the day came when the old woman passed away. The sons took over everything, but it was the older brother who took charge of the pot of gold for he was the wisest. If ever they needed anything for the farming or the fishing he would go to the pot and take a coin and it never seemed to empty.

But the younger brother became bitter. He wanted to have the same rights to the pot of gold. He began to complain that he always had to ask to buy this or pay for that, but in truth he was a fool and not trustworthy. More and more he came to resent his older brother and more and more they quarrelled.

One day when the older brother was away his younger sibling went to the pot and took all the gold coins. He wasted them on wares that neither he nor his brother needed. When the elder brother came home and found what had happened he ran to the pot and lifted the stone, but it was empty. Weep and wail and beg forgiveness as the young brother did, the well was dry. Never did the little clay pot yield another gold coin.

They say the two brothers fought and argued and never prospered more. Slowly the whole place fell to rack and ruin and was eventually abandoned. The lesson is very simple – never take more gold from the pot than you need. You cannot just find another one at the end of a rainbow!

THE VIKING WITH RATHLIN ROOTS

This the first of four stories with comparable plots and outcomes. It was obviously a strong theme among Rathlin storytellers. Did these folk tales have a common root or were there multiple instances of island children being stolen or otherwise taken away? That Viking and islander blood was mixed can be beyond doubt. Could it be that some of these stories evolved as euphemisms of a type to account for instances where Rathlin women gave birth to children fathered by Vikings – pillaging or otherwise? It is strange that there seem to be no stories dealing directly with a situation that must have arisen. (R80.17. 17/2/80)

Not for the first time or the last, Vikings brought bloodshed and tragedy to Rathlin. Their leader slaughtered the entire household of an island chief and thought them all dead when he heard the whimpering of a baby. When he peered into a crib he discovered a girl child only a few months old. Having a son near the same age, the brute might have felt some remorse or compassion. Whatever went through the warrior's mind, he took the child and carried her back to Lochlainn, where she was reared along with his son.

She was always told she was a foundling and not family but was otherwise treated well and brought up according to Viking tradition. Being of good breeding, the Viking betrothed her to his son and in the fullness of time they were bound together as man and wife. As time passed the woman gave birth to her own children, and she told them beautiful tales of a faraway island and of the people who lived there, such as she had heard the old Vikings tell. In time, her daughters became wives and her sons were schooled as warriors.

Many years later and the Norsemen came back to Rathlin. By this time, the old Viking's grandson had come of age and he led the raid. As was their way, the Norsemen pillaged and raped and slaughtered all before them. Wild-eyed and stirred by all the bloodletting and killing, the grandson broke down the door of a fine dwelling. The family inside cowered and trembled with fear. Sword in hand, he entered with a fearsome cry like a man possessed. But when he looked into the eyes of the people something deep in the pit of his stomach turned over and his heart leapt to his throat. The fierce lust for blood that was on him seemed to melt away in that instant. He found himself weakening and he dropped his sword arm to his side. For what seemed like an eternity, the people stared into his tear-filled eyes before he backed out of that house and left them in peace.

The Viking was greatly troubled by this strange happening, but he told no one because he felt weak and ashamed. Only when he returned to Lochlainn did he consult his elders and wisemen.

'You must return to Rachery,' they said, 'to the very same dwelling and put everyone there, man, woman and child to the sword without mercy. Do this and the demon within you will be banished.'

A year and a day later, the Viking returned to Rathlin. He went straight to the dwelling and broke in the door. The people within remembered their tormentor and again they cowered, but the same strange feeling came over the Norseman. He could not bring himself to cause any harm to those he had come to kill.

Sensing the Viking's distress and seeing the doubt in his eyes, the people were heartened. To appease him further, they ventured to offer their most cherished belongings, but he refused them. They offered food and drink in friendship and this time the Viking was overcome. His sword dropped from his hand, and he accepted their warmth and welcome. As he sat down to dine with them each began to tell their stories. Bit by bit it dawned on the young Viking that his mother had been stolen away by his grandfather all those years before. Through her, he was kith and kin to the very people he had once meant to slaughter.

What became of the Viking is not remembered but it seems that the people of Rathlin did not fear the coming of the Norsemen for many years to come. Ever after it was always said on the island that blood was indeed thicker than water – most of the time, anyway.

THE WARRIOR WOMAN

Modern listeners and readers of certain folk tales often find details like those of arranged marriages and the treatment of women in general objectionable. It must be remembered, however, that these stories reflect the realities of their time and would be less powerful if such detail were to be omitted. That said, the ending of this story was unnecessarily bleak, to my mind. The suggestion of a less dismal possibility affords a little more hope and might also serve as an antidote to the chauvinism inherent in the story. (R81.60. 27/2/81)

When the Vikings came raiding down through the islands of Skye, Iona and Islay and onwards towards Ireland, they lost warriors in skirmishes here and there. Often they would land on Rathlin to outfit their longboats and replenish their crews. Better it was for the islanders if the chieftains did not have to be forced into supplying provisions and men. To sweeten the dealings, payment in gold was sometimes offered by the Norsemen. Oftentimes, those who were taken away were killed in battle, drowned or absorbed into the Viking way of life and never saw Rathlin again.

One time longboats came to Rathlin. Their captain asked the chieftains for men. Never keen to hand over good warriors whatever the price, more favourable settlements were always sought. Fearing that his clan might be weakened and overwhelmed by the other island clans, one old wily chief complained to the Viking.

'I only have two young sons and no warriors to spare.'

'I will have only one of your sons then,' said the Viking menacingly.

'You will be in need on your return also. Come to me on your way back north and I will let you have one of my children.'

The Viking captain could see the old man's wisdom and agreed. For his part, the Rathlin chief wished his tormentor would be killed in battle and never return to hold him to the bargain.

Months passed and in the autumn sails appeared from the west. The Norsemen were returning. The old chief dreaded their arrival, for he had given his word and the Viking would surely not let him forget.

'I have come for what you promised me,' said the Norseman.

'And yet I still have no warriors to spare,' answered the chief. 'But wait! I do not break my word. I have a child. Take it, for a few paltry gold coins, and into the bargain I will give you a woman to nurse it.'

The Viking considered the deal. Having done well for himself and lost few men since last he was on Rathlin, he agreed. The child was wrapped in linen and woollen blankets and, carried by the woman, was taken north to Lochlainn.

It wasn't long after the Viking got home that he discovered the child was a girl. He had been duped by the Rathlin chieftain, who had handed over his own baby daughter. She was only a burden to him, who would one day have to be married off to some other chieftain's son, and all at the expense of a dowry of land and riches. The island chief thought himself well rid of her and was pleased that he had so easily played the Norseman.

The Viking's first instinct was to dash the child's brains out on a rock, for as a girl she was of no value to him either. He had hoped that the child would grow to become a great warrior chief like himself, but now he was made to look like a fool. If his men discovered the trick,

they would think their leader weak. With his pride wounded severely, he whispered a bitter oath of vengeance on the Rathlin chief. By the point of his sword the wet nurse was sworn to keep the secret and ordered to rear the child as a boy.

Such a harsh upbringing a child never received. As soon as she was able to stand a sword was put in her hand. She was taught to be fearless and cruel, and though she was always smaller and could never grow a beard, her cohorts never dared to tease her. No child ever grew up to be a better or more fearsome warrior. And all the while she believed herself to be of Viking blood for no one had ever revealed to her the truth.

Time passed and, disguised always as a man, the young woman led raids and returned time and again to her deceitful father with plunder and prisoners of whom to make slaves. Further and further she went and eventually came to Rathlin. She raided the island mercilessly but during her stay she spied a young man who caught her eye and ensnared her heart. For the first time in her life she felt tender feelings toward someone. It was a strange and unsettling sensation. Night after night she tossed and turned in her bed and dreamed about the young man. She resolved to return to the island to make peace and trade with the islanders. Her father saw the difference in her.

'I see a change in you my daughter,' He said to her one day, 'What is the reason for the softening of your warrior's heart?'

'I do not want to fight anymore father,' she said. 'I will return to Rachery and reveal myself to this man. If he will take me I will be his wife. If not, I will become an old hag.'

'Let me go ahead daughter, for this is a delicate matter and will need a light touch,' said the old Viking, and his unwitting, young charge agreed.

It didn't take long for the old Viking to discover that the object of his adopted daughter's affections was in fact her very own brother – the son of the Rathlin chieftain who had deceived him all those years before. The young man was already betrothed to another island woman. When he heard this, the old Viking began to devise the most vile and twisted act of revenge of which a mind could conceive.

'Warriors will soon be coming from the north,' he warned the young Rathlin man, 'Their cruel leader is intent on taking your bride to be. He is fearless, but you must defeat him or lose everything.'

Forewarned is forearmed, and the Rathlin warrior made his preparations for battle. He gathered his men, and as the Vikings landed he led a merciless attack. He singled out their leader – the small, slender figure with an unblemished boyish face. Even as his foe's open hands were raised to show goodwill, the Rathlin man lashed out without a moment's hesitation. It was only when the little Viking's torn garments were blown open by the wind and two lily white breasts were revealed, that everyone realised this most feared of warriors was little more than a slip of a girl.

Soon the whole truth came out as it always does in the end. When the young Rathlin man discovered that he had butchered his own flesh and blood – the sister from whom he had been separated so long before – he was distraught. Some say that in his terrible despair he took his own life. Others will tell you that he married his bride to be and together they had many children, and their daughters were just as cherished and loved as their sons.

THE STOLEN TWIN

This story contains very similar themes to that preceding but with a much clearer and happier ending. The main female character is manipulated almost as much by her male counterparts, but she is possessed of more agency than might be considered normal in the context of these folk tales. The story also seems to portray the ending of conflict and the beginnings of integration between Viking and islander. This could well have its basis in historical fact but was enacted over many years. (R80.32. 20/4/80)

When the very last Viking raid on Rathlin occurred no one remembers, but the story was often told how peace and harmony between the islanders and the men of Lochlainn finally came about.

For centuries the Vikings had raided and pillaged Rathlin. They raped women and killed anyone who stood against them. They stole livestock and crops and carried their captives away to be sold into slavery. Such were the brutal times in which they lived. But it was said there was one violation that even the Vikings shied away from – the slaughter of young children. The islanders knew this and so would often flee, leaving their youngest children to the mercy of the Norse raiders.

And so it happened to a family on Rathlin many years ago. The woman had given birth to twin girls a year before. Bad luck it was that the family should have been burdened with a daughter instead of a son who could fish and farm as he grew. But to have two girls to feed and rear and put aside dowries for was a heavy load to bear.

It was rare for twins to survive long in those far-off days. Some women wished for death to relieve them of the weakest one. A few even took matters into their own hands. But this woman could not bear to think such a thing. Her twins not only survived but thrived.

Then the Vikings came raiding once again. As they plundered the island their leader came across a cabin with the little twin girls wrapped up in a cradle. Their parents had left them in the hope that they at least would be spared. The Viking's wife had given him the sons he desired, but she craved a girl child for herself and so he took one of the twins as a gift for his woman. The other twin was left unharmed, and when her mother returned she was, truly, broken-hearted but her husband felt some relief that their burden had been lightened.

The stolen twin was taken back to Lochlainn and reared in the Viking household. She never knew anything different. She spoke their language, believed in their gods and loved her Viking family.

As she grew she began to have strange dreams about a small cabin on a beautiful island far across the sea where everyone knew her name, and of a sister with whom she shared everything. The dreams became so colourful and felt so real that they began to disturb her. Often she would wake in the morning to find herself weeping and with a deep yearning in her heart to find this place.

Years later, the stolen twin was married to a Viking chief. In time she gave birth to three sons and, but for her unsettling dreams, she was happy. One year towards the end of summer, her husband and his men returned from raiding in Ireland. They brought with them all kinds of plunder and a few captives from Rathlin. The Viking womenfolk gathered on the beach to greet their husbands and catch a glimpse of the new arrivals. As they unloaded the prisoners, one young man struggled against his captors, but manacled and chained as he was, he posed no threat. As he tramped up the beach he lifted his eyes and his gaze fell upon the stolen twin. The blood drained from his face, and he stopped in his tracks.

'Aintín, Aintín,' he called and then ran towards her.

She had learned enough of the Gaelic language from the many Irish slaves the Vikings kept to know what he was saying, 'Aunt, Aunt,' but she could make no sense of his meaning. Before he got near her, he was knocked to the ground and then dragged off, but again and again he cried, 'Aintín, Aintín.'

This troubled her greatly and once the new captives had settled down and been put to work as slaves, she went to this young man. Speaking to him in his native tongue, she asked him what he meant by his words.

'You are the living image of my mother,' he said. 'My grandmother has always talked about my mother's twin who was taken by the Vikings. They have always longed to know if you are alive or dead.'

'Tell me about my home and my family,' she begged with tears in her eyes, and as the young man spoke it was just as she had always seen in her dreams. Now everything made sense to her.

The stolen twin went to her Viking father and asked to be told the truth.

'I must know from where I came,' she said.

'You are my daughter,' he answered, 'And I warn you. Do not go down this path. No good will come of it.'

It was too late. The lid had been lifted on a box of secrets and could not be replaced. She begged to be allowed to go to Rathlin in a long-boat but neither her father nor husband would grant her permission.

The Irish slaves slept on an island out in the fjord to hinder their escape but came ashore each day to work according to their skills. Secretly the stolen twin spoke to the young Rathlin man and between them they set in motion a plan to escape. With his knowledge of boat building and her help in acquiring hides, he would build a currach. She would have to gather the food and drink they would need for the voyage and by the spring everything was ready. All they needed was some fair weather.

Early one morning the woman stole her three sons away and with enough men to man the currach and a Viking who was under pain of death to navigate, they set sail for Rathlin. It didn't take too long for them to be discovered and the woman's husband and his men followed in a longboat. But, favoured by the weather and it being light and well-handled, the currach could not be caught.

Several days and nights later, the dark, low shape of Rathlin came into view on the horizon. Before long the men were among their own people once again. After so many long years of separation, dreaming and wondering, the stolen twin was reunited with her sister and her mother – sadly her father had died years before. It was a tearful and happy homecoming but there was little time for rejoicing. A Viking longship was bearing down on the island and bloodshed was sure to follow.

Leaving her eldest son as a ransom, the stolen twin left her native island in the currach manned by her nephew and his comrades and headed north again. They met her husband on Islay. He was preparing for a merciless attack on Rathlin.

'If you want to see your eldest son again then no harm must come to these men who have helped me. They are my kin and kin to your children,' she told her husband.

Well, to cut a long story short, the whole truth was soon told. A settlement was agreed upon and not a drop of blood was to be spilled. The Viking's half-Rathlin Island son was safely returned to him, and he and his wife returned to Lochlainn. The Rathlin men who had been captured and enslaved were freed without harm to go back to their families.

As for the stolen twin, contented and no longer troubled by strange dreams, often it was that she came to visit her twin sister and her family on Rathlin. Whenever her husband and his men came, it was to trade and feast. Over the years many more blood ties were made, and the island was never raided again – not by Norsemen anyway.

THE EMBER, THE FALCON
AND THE WOLF

In essence, this is the same story as 'The Pot of Gold' but with much more colour and drama. The introduction of the 'three' gifts conforms to a folk tale convention found not just in Ireland. (In TC's version there are four gifts – the fourth being a cloak that would never wear out and always keep the woman warm. I omitted this as I felt it was almost a duplication of the ember that functioned in a similar way.) The power of three in storytelling is long established. It provides a universal balance, a pleasing rhythm and lists of three are more easily remembered by the oral teller. The imagery of the ember, the falcon and the wolf is also very striking! (R81.60. 27/2/81)

While the Norsemen ceased to raid Rathlin, other neighbouring clans did not, for indeed the island was now seen as a Viking refuge and the islanders their allies. One time, a ruthless chieftain from the mainland came over and was sorely punishing the islanders. When Viking sails appeared on the horizon the Norsemen were hailed as friends and saviours by the islanders. They rowed out to greet the longboats and pleaded for help. It was freely given, and a bloody battle ensued. Three days it lasted, but eventually the Vikings defeated the interlopers and drove what was left of them away back to the mainland. Peace fell over the island once more, but many lay dead and wounded.

The chief of the Vikings was badly injured and could not travel onwards with his men, for they were intent on raiding along the north coast of Hibernia. It was decided that he would stay with a Rathlin woman skilled in the old ways of healing. Her husband had been killed in the fighting and she was left with two sons to rear.

Despite the woman's care, the aged Viking did not recover well. When his men returned, a great storm blew their ships on past Rathlin and they could not land to collect him. It was many months before

they were able to come back. At long last they arrived but found their comrade ailing gravely.

'I am dying,' he said, 'I wish to return to Lochlainn to be buried with my ancestors.'

So, his men made preparations to carry out his wishes and set sail for their homeland. Before they left the old Viking wanted to bid farewell to the woman who had cared for him so long and so well.

'How might I repay your kindness?' he asked, for it was an old and dearly held Viking custom to settle any debt of goodwill generously.

'I am getting old,' she said, 'I do not need silver or gold.'

'Then what do you need?' said the Viking.

'To feel warm and well fed and safe in my bed at night. That is all an old woman wants.'

'Very well,' said the Viking, 'I will see to it.'

A year and a day later, his men returned to Rathlin with the sad news that their captain had died and was buried according to their ways. He had sent the woman three gifts: a burning ember that would never die, a huge white falcon that would fetch her food every day and a great grey wolf that would guard her cabin door at night.

And so, the woman lived in comfort with her two sons. Never did they want for a fire to heat themselves or cook their food. Fresh meat – grouse, duck, goose and hare – was theirs whenever they wanted it, fetched by the falcon every day. And at night the mighty wolf lay across their threshold and neither thief nor murderer dared to come near the place.

Eventually the old woman died in her old age and her two sons took charge of her gifts. Sad to say, they argued over them. The older son thought the ember, the falcon and the wolf to be of great value and wanted to trade them for gold. The younger son knew their true value and wanted to keep them.

The brothers quarrelled endlessly over who had the greater say, until one evening while they worked in a field of oats with reaping hooks, they fell to violence. Soon the younger brother lay mortally wounded. While his lifeblood was still seeping into the soil, his older sibling ran to their dead mother's cabin. There he found the ember had become a pile of cold grey ash, the white falcon had broken her tethers and flown away, and the wolf lay dead on the grave of his mistress.

A NATIVE SON RETURNED

This story has a plot reminiscent of the three preceding stories. Like the female characters in these stories, the rather innocent male protagonist here seems not to have much choice in his destiny, at least to begin with. In the end, however, he becomes the island's saviour – a variation on the archetype of the reluctant hero. In this tale is also found another example where Vikings repay a good deed and are shown to be possessed of compassion and kindness. (R81.60. 27/2/81)

It used to be that when Viking raiders were coming near to Rathlin they started up a heavy chanting that drifted low over the waves, louder and louder. It was a sound once dreaded by the islanders. After old feelings of ill will ceased, however, the Vikings still belted out a chorus in their own language as they came in to land. It had taken many years, but now this strange declaration of arrival came to be warmly welcomed by the Rathlin folk.

One time though, a longboat arrived in a gale of wind, and no one saw or heard them. The vessel was wrecked on the north side of the island. All the men on board got ashore but they were trapped at the foot of the steep cliffs. Days passed and their plight went unnoticed. Eventually a Rathlin fisherman braving the stormy weather saw them and raised the call for help.

The only way the Vikings could be saved was by rope from above, but they were so weakened by hunger and cold they could not make the hard climb without help. An islander who went after the sea birds' eggs at Kebble and was well known as a great climber went down on a long rope. One by one he raised the Norsemen on his back to safety. But one of their crew had died on the rocks and his comrades were loath to leave him. They begged the islander to bring their friend up that he might be given a fitting burial.

One last time the brave Rathlin man went down on the rope. Though his arms and legs ached and he was worn out, he heaved the dead Viking on to his back and began the long, hard climb back up.

As he neared the top, the fibrous rope gave way and he fell to his death on the rocks below. The Vikings and islanders alike were distraught, not least the poor Rathlin man's wife and her weakling son.

When the Vikings recovered their strength they built themselves a vessel to get home. Before they left, they went to the widow of the man who had saved them.

'Your husband gave his life for us,' their leader said, 'We are deeply indebted to him. Let us take your son to Lochlainn and we will make a warrior of him.'

Well, the woman glanced over at her skinny, hapless son whimpering in the corner for the loss of his father and she thought, 'I might as well let him go for he's only a burden to me as he is.'

'Very well,' she said, 'Take him and good luck to ye for he won't do any good here.'

Away the Vikings went, and many years passed before they were seen or heard tell of again. When they returned they found the island had been ravaged by clansmen from the mainland and the people were in great need of succour and someone to lead them.

Ashore came the widow's son. He had a mighty sword at his side and men under his command. He went to see his old mother, but she barely recognised him, so altered was he. Underneath his fine woollen cloak held in place by a pin at his breast were broad shoulders and thickly muscled arms more like those of his long-dead father. He had a chest like an oak barrel and a roar like a bull. The Vikings had trained him well in weaponry and warfare and he had indeed become a fearless warrior. There and then, he installed himself as chieftain of the island and set about ridding it of vermin.

Not while he lived was Rathlin ever troubled by plundering wayfarers again and the island was always a welcome sanctuary to his comrades from the north.

FURTHER READING

Campbell, Mary, *Sea Wrack, Long-ago Tales of Rathlin Island* (J.S. Scarlett & Sons, 1951).

Clark, Wallace, *Rathlin – Disputed Island* (Volturna Press, 1971).

Cecil, Tommy, *The Harsh Winds of Rathlin* (Impact Printing, 1990).

Dickson, J. Margret/Mrs Gage (1851), *A History of the Island of Rathlin*, (Impact Printing, 1995).

Ballard, Linda-May, 'Seal Stories and Beliefs on Rathlin Island'. *Ulster Folklife*, Vol. 29 (1983).

Ballard, Linda-May, *Forgetting Frolic: Marriage Traditions in Ireland*, Queen's University of Belfast (Institute of Irish Studies, 1998).

Urwin, Colin, *The Iron Hag and Other Stories from the Sam Henry Collection* (Causeway Museum Services, 2023).

Urwin, Colin, *Irish Folk Tales of Coast and Sea* (The History Press, 2024).

McBride, Jack, *Traveller in The Glens* (Appletree Press, 1979).

McCurdy, Augustine, *Stories and Legends of Rathlin*, (Impact Printing, 2006).

Watson, Philip, *Rathlin Nature & Folklore* (Stone Country, 2011).